John McGahern was born in Dublin in 1934 and brought up in the Republic of Ireland. He trained to be a primary-school teacher before becoming a full-time writer, and later taught and travelled extensively. He lived in County Leitrim. The author of six highly acclaimed novels and four collections of short stories, he was the recipient of numerous awards and honours, including a Society of Authors Travelling Scholarship, the American-Irish Award, the Prix Etrangère Ecureuil and the Chevalier de l'Ordre des Arts et des Lettres. *Amongst Women*, which won both the GPA and the *Irish Times* Award, was shortlisted for the Booker Prize and made into a four-part BBC television series. His work appeared in numerous anthologies and has been translated into many languages. In 2005, his autobiography, *Memoir*, won the South Bank Literature Award. John McGahern died in 2006.

JOHN McGAHERN

Amongst Women

faber and faber

First published in 1991
by Faber and Faber Limited
Bloomsbury House, 74–77 Great Russell Street,
London WC1B 3DA
Open Market paperback edition 1990
This paperback edition first published in 2008

Phototypeset by Input Typesetting Ltd, London
Printed and bound in Great Britain by
CPI Group (UK) Ltd, Croydon, CR0 4YY

A CIP record for this book is available
from the British Library

ISBN 978-0-571-22564-4

For Madeline

As he weakened, Moran became afraid of his daughters. This once powerful man was so implanted in their lives that they had never really left Great Meadow, in spite of jobs and marriages and children and houses of their own in Dublin and London. Now they could not let him slip away.

'You'll have to shape up, Daddy. You can't go on like this. You're giving us no help. We can't get you better on our own.'

'Who cares? Who cares anyhow?'

'We care. We all care very much.'

They all came at Christmas. After Christmas, Mona, the one girl who had not married, came every weekend from Dublin. Sometimes Sheila got away from her family to come with her and she drove down for a few hours as well as now and again in the middle of the week. The air fare from London was too expensive for Maggie to come regularly. Michael, their younger brother, had promised to come from London at Easter but Luke, the eldest, still would not come. All three girls planned to come to revive Monaghan Day. They had to explain to their stepmother Rose what Monaghan Day was. She had never heard of it in all her time in the house.

The end-of-February fair in Mohill was Monaghan Day. McQuaid came every year to the house on Monaghan Day. He and Moran had fought in the same flying column in the war. McQuaid always drank a bottle of whiskey in the house when he came.

'If we could revive Monaghan Day for Daddy it could help to start him back to himself. Monaghan Day meant the world to him once.'

'I'm sure Daddy was far from delighted to see a bottle of whiskey drank in the house,' Rose was doubtful about the whole idea.

'He never minded McQuaid drinking the whiskey. You wouldn't get McQuaid to the house without whiskey.'

They clung so tenaciously to the idea that Rose felt she couldn't stand in their way. Moran was not to be told. They wanted it to come as a sudden surprise – jolt. Against all reason they felt it could turn his slow decline around like a Lourdes' miracle. Forgotten was the fearful nail-biting exercise Monaghan Day had always been for the whole house; with distance it had become large, heroic, blood-mystical, something from which the impossible could be snatched.

Maggie flew over from London on the morning of the Day. Mona and Sheila met her at Dublin Airport and the three sisters drove to Great Meadow in Mona's car. They did not hurry. With the years they had drawn closer. Apart, they could be breathtakingly sharp on the others' shortcomings but together their individual selves gathered into something very close to a single presence.

On the tides of Dublin or London they were hardly more than specks of froth but together they were the aristocratic Morans of Great Meadow, a completed world, Moran's daughters. Each scrap of news any one of them had about themselves or their immediate family – child, husband, dog, cat, Bendix dishwasher, a new dress or pair of shoes, the price of every article they bought – was as fascinating to each other as if it were their very own; and any little thing out of Great Meadow was pure binding. Together they were the opposite of women who will nod and nod as they pretend to listen to another, waiting for the first pause of breath to muscle in with the growing pains and glories of their own house, the impatience showing on their faces as they wait. Mullingar was passed and they felt they had hardly said a word to one another. At the hotel in Longford they broke the journey to have tea and sandwiches, and just as the winter light began to fail they were turning in the open gate under the poisonous yew tree.

In spite of their wish to make the visit a surprise, Rose had told Moran they were arriving.

'They must think I'm on the way out.'

'The opposite,' she reassured. 'But they think you should be getting far better.'

'How can they all manage to get away together like that?'

'It must have fallen that way. Isn't it worth getting dressed up for once?'

'Who cares now anyhow?' he said automatically but changed into his brown suit. His face was flushed with excitement when they came.

In their nervousness they offered at once the gifts they had brought: tea, fruit, duty-free whiskey – 'It'll be useful to have in the house even if nobody drinks it and we might need a glass' – a printed silk headscarf, thick fur gloves.

'What did you want to bring anything to me for?' He always disliked having to accept presents.

'You were complaining at Christmas that your hands were always cold, Daddy.'

As if to turn attention away from the continual coldness of his hands, he pulled on the gloves comically and pretended to grope about the room with them like a blind man.

'The gloves are only for when you go out. I'm afraid all this excitement is going to your head, Daddy.' Rose, laughing, took the gloves away as he pretended to need them to wear about the house.

'I haven't discovered yet what brought out all the troops,' he said when the laughing stopped.

'Don't you remember the day it is? Monaghan Day! The day when McQuaid always used to come from the fair in Mohill and we had to make the big tea.'

'What's that got to do with anything?' Just as he resented gifts he resented any dredging up of the past. He demanded that the continuing present he felt his life to be should not be shadowed or challenged.

'We thought it was as good an excuse as any and we were all able to get away at the same time. So here we are.'

'It was a poor excuse then. McQuaid was a drunken black-guard who was with me in the war. I felt sorry for him. If I didn't give him a square meal on Monaghan Day he'd drink himself stupid in Mohill.'

'They've come all this way to see you and is that all the welcome they get,' Rose chided gently. 'Who cares about poor McQuaid, God rest him, he's long gone.'

'Who cares about anything now anyhow?' he demanded.

'We care. We care very much. We love you.'

'God help your wits then. Pay no attention to me. I wrote to that older brother of yours, "My capabilities are of little matter now", but I suppose I might be as well off writing to myself for all the answer I'm likely to get.'

He went silent and dark and withdrew into himself, the two thumbs rotating about one another as he sat in the car chair by the fire. A quick glance between Rose and the girls was enough for them to know that it was better to make no mention of their elder brother. They began to busy themselves cheerfully with preparations for the meal, one or other of them constantly trying to engage Moran with this small thing or that, until he was drawn by their uncanny tact into the general cheerfulness. When they finally sat down to the meal it was Moran himself who brought McQuaid back into the day.

'McQuaid wasn't a bad sort but he was misfortunate with the drink. The interesting thing about him is that he was one of those people who always turn out to be lucky no matter what they do. When he started to buy he knew nothing about cattle. Yet he made a fortune. Those people always get on better in the world than decent men.'

'His great hour was when he dressed up as the newspaper boy and went to meet the train,' Sheila said tentatively. She had heard it every year on Monaghan Day for years but she was unsure if Moran would allow any talk of the war. He generally went stone-silent whenever it was mentioned.

'He was lucky in that too and he had no nerves.'

4

'He always said you were the whole brains of the column. That everything they ever went into was planned by you, down to the last detail,' Mona was emboldened to add.

'I'd gone to school longer than the others. To the Latin school in Moyne. I could read maps, calculate distances. You'd never think it but McQuaid, like many of the others, was more or less illiterate though he could add and subtract quick enough when it concerned his pocket. It was easy to get the name of brains in those days.'

As if he suddenly wanted to return the girls' favour on this Monaghan Day, he spoke to them openly about the war for the first time in their lives. 'The English didn't seem to know right what they were doing. I think they were just going through the motions of what had worked before. Look at the train business. Imagine having a brass band meet a colonel in the middle of the bogs with the whole countryside up in arms. A child wouldn't do it.

'Don't let anybody fool you. It was a bad business. We didn't shoot at women and children like the Tans but we were a bunch of killers. We got very good but there was hardly a week when some of us wasn't killed. Of the twenty-two men in the original column only seven were alive at the Truce. We were never sure we'd be alive from one day to the next. Don't let them pull wool over your eyes. The war was the cold, the wet, standing to your neck in a drain for a whole night with bloodhounds on your trail, not knowing how you could manage the next step toward the end of a long march. That was the war: not when the band played and a bloody politician stepped forward to put flowers on the ground.

'What did we get for it? A country, if you'd believe them. Some of our own johnnies in the top jobs instead of a few Englishmen. More than half of my own family work in England. What was it all for? The whole thing was a cod.'

'They say you should have gone to the very top in the army after the war but you were stopped. McQuaid always said they set out to stop you,' Sheila said with borrowed vehemence.

'I was stopped all right but it wasn't as simple as poor

5

McQuaid made out. In an army in peacetime you have to arse-lick and know the right people if you want to get on. I was never any good at getting on with people. You should all know that by now,' he said half humorously.

There were tears in the girls' eyes as they tried to smile back. Rose was quiet and watchful.

'For people like McQuaid and myself the war was the best part of our lives. Things were never so simple and clear again. I think we never rightly got the hang of it afterwards. It was better if it had never happened. Tired now. You were all great girls to travel such distances to see one sick old man.'

He took his beads from the small purse. They hung loose from his hand. 'Anyhow it no longer matters to you or to me, but whoever has the last laugh in the whole business is going to have to spend a hell of a length of time laughing. *We* have to try to work as best we can and *pray*.'

He looked so strained and tired that they offered to say the Rosary in his room but he brushed the offer aside. He knelt as erect as ever at the table.

'Thou, O Lord, wilt open my lips,' he called. When he came to the Dedication he paused as if searching. Then, in a sudden flash that he was sometimes capable of, he acknowledged his daughters' continuing goodwill and love, love that usually he seemed inherently unable to return. 'Tonight we offer up this Holy Rosary for the repose of the soul of James McQuaid.'

When the prayers were ended the three girls kissed him goodnight in turn, and Rose went with him to their room. The girls started to wash up and tidy; very soon the litter of the evening was cleared away, the room made ready for breakfast.

When Rose saw the table already set for morning, she said, 'If you were around for too long I'd be spoiled rotten. I don't know what anybody else is having but I'm going to be bad tonight and have a cigarette and hot whiskey. You all took Daddy out of himself tonight. That all of you managed to come meant the world to Daddy.'

The next morning they were idling in the luxury of a long breakfast, enjoying the chatting in the warmth of the room, the

6

tussocks in the white field outside the window stiff with frost, the only green grass the huge dark circles under the cypress trees, when a single shotgun blast came from the front room. They looked at one another in fear, moving quickly as one person to the room. He was standing at the open window in his pyjamas, the shotgun in his hand, staring out at the front field where the black splash of a jackdaw lay on the white ground beneath the ash tree.

'Are you all right, Daddy?' they called out.

When it was clear that he was, Rose cried, 'You frightened the life out of us, Daddy.'

'That bloody bird has been annoying me for days.'

'You'll get your death of cold standing there at the open window,' Maggie complained and Rose brought the window down.

'You didn't miss anyhow.' Rose was intent on laughing away the incongruity of the situation.

'I don't think Daddy ever missed,' Mona said.

'The closest I ever got to any man was when I had him in the sights of the rifle and I never missed.' The voice was so absent and tired that it took some of the chill from the words.

He allowed Rose to take the gun away but not before he had removed the empty shell. He dressed and had breakfast with them at the table. The gun was returned to its usual place in the corner of the room and no more mention was made of the dead jackdaw.

'Tired again,' he said simply after an hour and went back to his room.

Maggie was taking a plane to London that night and Sheila and Mona were driving her to the airport. The two girls would not be back till the following weekend. Moran stood with Rose in the doorway watching the car drive away. He waved weakly after the car but he did not speak as Rose shut the door and they turned back into the house.

Monaghan Day had revived nothing but a weak fanciful ghost of what had been. After Easter and many other alarms, when none of the girls was able to be in Great Meadow, Rose had her sister buy a brown Franciscan habit in the town. In spite of the hush and emptiness of the house, the two women smuggled the habit in like thieves and later that evening Rose hid it among her most intimate articles of clothing in a part of the wardrobe that Moran never opened.

The attempt to revive Monaghan Day was a gesture as weak as a couple who marry in order to try to retrieve a lost relationship, the mind having changed the hard actual fact into what was comfortable to feel.

On the last Monaghan Day that McQuaid came to the house Moran was on edge as he waited for him as he had been on edge every Monaghan Day, the only day in the year that McQuaid came to Great Meadow. Since morning he had been in and out of the kitchen where Maggie and Mona were cleaning and tidying and preparing for the big meal. Though Maggie was eighteen, tall and attractive, she was still as much in awe of Moran as when she had been a child. Mona, two years younger, was the more likely to clash with him, but this day she agreed to be ruled by Maggie's acquiescence. Sheila, a year younger still, was too self-centred and bright ever to challenge authority on poor ground and she pretended to be sick in order to escape the tension of the day. Alone, the two girls were playful as they went about their tasks, mischievous at times, even carefully boisterous; but as soon as their father came in they would sink into a beseeching drabness, cower as close to being invisible as they could.

'How do the lamb chops look?' he demanded again. 'Are these the best lamb chops you could get? Haven't I told you time in and time out never – never – to get lamb chops anywhere but from Kavanagh's? Has everything to be drummed in a hundred times? God, why is nothing ever made clear in this house? Everything has to be dragged out of everybody.'

'Kavanagh said the steak wasn't great but that the lamb was good,' Maggie added but Moran was already on his way out again, muttering that not even simple things were made clear

8

in this house and if simple things couldn't be made clear how was a person ever to get from one day to the next in this world.

The two girls were quiet for a long time after the door closed; then suddenly, unaccountably, they started to push one another, boisterously mimicking Moran: 'God, O God, what did I do to deserve such a crowd? Gawd, O Gawd, not even the simple things are made clear,' falling into chairs laughing.

A loud imperious knocking came on the tongued boards of the ceiling in the middle of the rowdy relief. They stopped to listen and as they did the knocking stopped.

'She's no more sick than my big toe. Whenever there's a whiff of trouble she takes to her bed with the asthma. She has books and sweets hidden up there,' Mona said. They waited in silence until the knocking resumed, insistent and angry.

'Boohoo!' they responded. 'Boohoo! Boohoo! Boohoo!' The knocking made the boards of the ceiling tremble. She was using a boot or shoe. 'Boohoo!' they echoed. 'Boohoo! Boohoo! . . .'

The stairs creaked. In a moment Sheila stood angrily framed in the doorway. 'I've been knocking for ages and all ye do is laugh up at me.'

'We never heard. We'd laugh up at nobody.'

'Ye heard only too well. I'm going to tell Daddy on the pair of ye.'

'Boohoo!' they repeated.

'You think I'm joking. You'll pay for this before it's over.'

'What do you want?'

'I'm sick and you won't even bring up a drink.'

They gave her a jug of barley water and a clean glass.

'You know what day it is and McQuaid is coming from the mart. He's in and out like a devil. You can't expect us to dance attendance up the stairs as well. If he comes in and sees you like that in the door he'll have something to say,' Maggie said but Sheila slipped back upstairs before she finished.

They draped the starched white tablecloth over the big deal table. The room was wonderfully warm, the hotplate of the stove glowing a faint orange. They began to set the table, growing relaxed and easy, enjoying the formality of the room, when

Moran came in again from the fields. This time he stood in the centre of the room, plainly unsure as to what had brought him in, his eye searching around for something to fasten on, like someone in mid-speech forgetting what they had to say.

'Is everything all right?'

'Everything is all right, Daddy.'

'Be sure the chops are well done,' he said and went out again. No sooner had the door closed than Mona, released from the tension of his presence, let slip a plate from her hands. They stood watching dumbly in horrible fascination after it shattered. Quickly they swept up the pieces and hid them away, wondering how they would replace the plate without being found out.

'Don't worry,' Maggie comforted Mona who was still pale with shock. 'We'll find some way round it.' They were too sick at heart to mimic or mock this mood away. Anything broken had to be hidden until it could be replaced or forgotten.

Outside it was cold but there was no rain. It was always cold on Monaghan Day, the traditional day poor farmers sold their winter stock and the rich farmers bought them for fattening. Moran was neither rich nor poor but his hatred and fear of poverty was as fierce as his fear of illness which meant that he would never be poor but that he and all around him would live as if they were paupers. Moran had no work in the fields but still he stayed outside in the cold, looking at hedges, examining walls, counting cattle. He was too excited to be able to stay indoors. As the light began to fail he retreated into the shelter of the fir plantation to watch the road for McQuaid's car. If McQuaid had a big order to fill he mightn't come till after dark.

The light was almost gone when the white Mercedes came slowly along the road and turned into the open gate under the yew tree. Moran did not move even after the car stopped. In fact, he instinctively stepped backwards into the plantation as the car door was thrown open. Without moving he watched McQuaid struggle from the car and then stand leaning on the open door as if waiting for someone to appear. He could have called out from where he stood but he did not. McQuaid slammed the car door and walked towards the house. Not until he was several minutes within the house did Moran leave the plantation. He came slowly and deliberately across the fields to the back door. Though he had lived for weeks for this hour he now felt a wild surge of resentment towards McQuaid as he came into his own house.

McQuaid was seated in the armchair by the fire. His powerful trunk and huge belly filled the chair and the yellow cattleman's boots were laced halfway up the stout legs. He did not rise from the chair or acknowledge Moran's entrance in any way except to direct the flirting banter he was having with the girls to Moran.

'These girls are blooming. You better have your orchards well fenced or you'll be out of apples by October.'

The words were said with such good humour and aggressive sureness that it would have been impossible to take offence. Moran hardly heard; all resentment left him as quickly as it had come: McQuaid was here and it was Monaghan Day.

'Michael.' McQuaid reached out of the chair and took Moran's hand in a firm grip.

'Jimmy.' Moran responded with the same simplicity. 'Have you been here long?'

'Not long. I had a fine talk with these girls. They are great girls.'

Moran walked across to the curtained press where he kept medicines and took out a glass and a full bottle of Redbreast. He poured out a large measure of the whiskey and brought it to McQuaid. Maggie placed a jug of spring water on the table. 'Say when,' Moran poured the water into the glass. McQuaid held out the glass until it was three-quarters full.

'You'll need it after the mart,' Moran said.

'I don't need it but I'll do much better than that. I'll enjoy it. Good luck everybody.'

'How did it go?' Moran asked with a heartiness that didn't suit him.

'The same as every other Monaghan Day,' McQuaid said.

'Was it good or bad?' Moran continued.

'It was neither good nor bad. It was money. All the farmers

11

think their cattle are special but all I ever see is money. If a beast is around or below a certain sum of money I buy. If it goes over that I'm out.'

'I've often watched you in the past and wondered how you know exactly the right time to enter the bidding, the right time to leave,' Moran praised. His fascination with McQuaid's mastery of his own world was boyish. He had never been able to deal with the outside. All his dealings had been with himself and that larger self of family which had been thrown together by marriage or accident: he had never been able to go out from his shell of self.

'I don't know how I know that,' McQuaid said. 'All I know is that it cost me a lot of money to learn.'

The girls had the freshly cut bread, butter and milk on the table. The lamb chops sizzled as they were dropped into the big pan. The sausages, black pudding, bacon, halves of tomatoes were added soon after to the sides of the pan. The eggs were fried in a smaller pan. Mona scalded the large teapot and set it to brew. The two girls were silent as they cooked and when they had to speak to one another spoke in quick, urgent whispers.

'This looks like a meal fit for a king. It makes me want to roll up my sleeves,' McQuaid said in praise and plain enjoyment at the prospect of it as the plates were put on the table. He finished his glass of whiskey with a flourish before rising from the chair.

The two men ate in silence, with relish, waited on by the two girls. As soon as McQuaid pushed his empty plate contentedly aside he said, 'These are great girls but where are the missing soldiers?'

'Sheila is upstairs with a cold,' Maggie pointed to the ceiling. 'And Michael is gone to our aunt in the mountains for a week.'

'Where's Luke then?'

The girls looked from McQuaid to Moran and back to McQuaid again but they did not speak.

'We don't know where he is,' Moran said reluctantly. He particularly disliked parting with information about the house.

12

'You couldn't open your mouth in this house before he left but he'd be down your throat.'

'If I know you I'd warrant he was given his money's worth,' McQuaid laughed gently and when Moran didn't answer he added, 'The young will have their way, Michael. Anyhow I always liked Luke. He is very straight and manly.'

'I respect all my children equally,' Moran said. 'How are your lads?'

'You know they're all married now. I don't see much of them unless they want something and they don't see much of me. They're good lads though. They work long hours.'

'And the good lady?'

'Oh, the old dosey's all right. She needs plenty of shouting at or she'd go to sleep on her feet.'

They had married young and their three sons married young as well. They lived alone now in the big cattle dealer's house with the white railing in the middle of fields. He was seldom in the house except to eat or sleep and when he was all he ever did was yell, 'Get the tea. Polish the boots. Kick out that bloody cat. Get me a stud. Where's the fucking collar?' 'In a minute, Jimmy. Coming. On the way. It's here in my very hand,' his wife would race and flurry and call. Then he would be gone for days. She would spoil her cats, read library books and tend her garden and the riotous rockery of flowers along the south wall of the house that he encouraged the cattle to eat. After days of peace the door would crash open: 'There's six men here with lorries. Put on the kettle. Set the table. Get hopping. Put wheels under yourself. We're fucking starving!' There was never a hint of a blow. So persistent was the language that it had become no more remarkable than just another wayward manner of speaking and their sons paid so little attention to it that it might well have been one of the many private languages of love.

The dishes had been washed and put away. Mona went to join Sheila upstairs. Maggie was going visiting. Another night Moran would have questioned her but not tonight.

Years ago Moran loaned McQuaid money when he had

started in the cattle business but now McQuaid was the richer and more powerful man and they saw little of one another. They came together once a year to slip back into what McQuaid said were the days of their glory. Moran was too complicated to let anybody know what he thought of anything. Moran had commanded a column in the war. McQuaid had been his lieutenant. From year to year they used the same handrails to go down into the past: lifting the cartwheel at the crossroads, the drilling sessions by the river, the first ambush, marching at night between the safe houses, the different characters in the houses, the food, the girls . . . The interrogation of William Taylor the spy and his execution by the light of a paraffin lantern among his own cattle in the byre. The Tans had swarmed over the countryside looking for them after the execution. They had lived for a while in holes cut in the turf banks. The place was watched night and day. Once the British soldiers came on Mary Duignan when she was bringing them tea and sandwiches. The Duignans were so naturally pale-faced that Mary showed no sign that anything was other than normal and she continued to bring tea and sandwiches to men working on a further turf bank. Seeing the British soldiers, the startled men sat and ate though they had just risen from a complete meal.

'Mary was a topper,' McQuaid said with emotion. 'Only for Mary that day our goose was cooked. She was a bloody genius to think of giving the food to the men on the bank. She's married to a carpenter in Dublin now. She has several children.'

Moran poured more whiskey into the empty glass.

'Are you sure you won't chance a drop?' McQuaid raised his glass. 'It's no fun drinking on your own.'

'I couldn't handle it,' Moran said. 'You know that. I had to give it up. Now I couldn't look at it.'

'I shouldn't have asked you then.'

'I don't mind. I don't mind at all.'

The reminiscing continued – the deaths of friends, one man marching alone through the night, the terrible hard labour it was for some men to die, night marches from one safe house to another, the rain, the wet, the damp, the cold of waiting for an ambush in one place for hours.

'We had them on the run by then. They were afraid to venture out except in convoys.'

'People who would have spat in our faces three years before were now clapping our backs. They were falling over one another to get on the winning side.'

'Many of them who had pensions and medals and jobs later couldn't tell one end of a gun from the other. Many of the men who had actually fought got nothing. An early grave or the emigrant ship. Sometimes I get sick when I see what I fought for,' Moran said.

'It makes no sense your not taking the IRA pension. You earned it. You could still have it in the morning,' McQuaid said.

'I'd throw it in their teeth,' Moran clenched and unclenched his hands as he spoke.

'I never question the colour of any man's money. If I'm offered it I take it,' but Moran was too consumed to respond and McQuaid went on. 'Then it began to get easier. We hadn't to hide any longer. One hot day I remember leaving guns and clothes along the river bank and swimming without a stitch on. Another Sunday we went trolling, dragging an otter behind the boat. Then they tried to bring in the general.'

'He wasn't a general. He was a trumped-up colonel.'

'Whatever he was we settled his hash,' McQuaid gloated. 'You had a great head on you the way you thought the plan through from beginning to end. You've been wasted ever since.'

'Without you it would never have worked. You were as cool as if you were out for a stroll,' Moran said.

'You could plan. You worked it out from beginning to end. None of the rest of us had that kind of head.'

'We had spies. We had men in the town for weeks. They were bringing the big fellow in on the three o'clock train. They were going to put on the big show. They had a band and a guard of honour outside the station, their backs to a row of railwaymen's cottages. They never checked the cottages.'

'They wouldn't have found us anyhow.'

'Nibs McGovern met that train every day with his trolley to pick up the papers and the Boland loaves that the shops got for special customers. He was such a fixture that no one noticed him any more. It fell into our hands.'

'Looking back on it the plan couldn't have been simpler but we must have rehearsed it forty times. We all slipped into town after dark. Only Tommy Flood, the solicitor's clerk, gave any trouble.'

'Then we nabbed Nibs,' McQuaid laughed. 'Just as he was getting ready to go out on the town. We were lucky there as well. Nibs didn't go to any one pub in particular. Nibs was no trouble. He could think quick enough when he had to. We gave him whiskey and hadn't to tie him up till the morning and that was only for his own good.'

'Then there was the waiting,' Moran said violently.

'I'll never forget it. Dressed up in Nibs's gear,' McQuaid said. 'The clothes were fit to stand up on their own, they were that stiff with dust and grease. The waiting was terrible. It's like getting old. Nothing happens and then the whole bloody thing is on top of you before you know it. The Tommies marching to the station. The band. Sound of the train getting closer and before I knew it I was out on that street pushing the trolley. The wheels were so loose I was afraid they'd fall off. The one thing we never thought of was to check the wheels. The overcoat was buttoned over the gun and the grenade. Even in the middle of summer Nibs wore that overcoat.'

'I had the stopwatch on you from behind one of the windows. I followed every step. I was afraid you'd get to the slope too soon. I was afraid you could run into our fire if you got too far up on the slope.'

'The gates were closed. The train came puffing in. The fucking band struck up "God Save the King". There were three fir trees beside the platform. They said they never grew right because of the smoke and steam. The sergeant major was shouting. They were all standing to attention. The colonel or general or whatever he was came down the platform. There was another officer with him holding a sword upright. I kept pushing the

16

trolley, praying to Jesus the bloody wheels wouldn't come loose. No one even looked at me or the trolley. The pair came along inspecting the troops. The one holding the sword was young. The colonel was a big stoutish man with red eyebrows. All I remember thinking of as I pushed the trolley and looked at the red face and eyebrows was, My friend, you are about to take the longest journey a man ever takes in this life. He took the full blast. The other man was still holding the sword upright as he went down. I pulled the pin out of the grenade. The line of soldiers was still half standing to attention when I went through them. I hadn't to use the revolver. As soon as I got to the other side of the bank I threw myself down and started to roll.'

'That's all I was watching for. As soon as I saw you go down I gave the order to fire,' Moran said. 'Some of them were still standing to attention as they fell. They hadn't a clue where the fire was coming from. Then a few soldiers up at the goods store fired into their own men.'

'By the time I rolled to the bottom of the slope I could see the steady fire coming from the windows. I waited to get my breath before cutting across the road. I don't think I was fired on once. The first thing I did when I got behind the houses was to get out of Nibs's clothes.'

'They were beginning to fire back from behind the station. Michael Sweeney was hit in the shoulder. I gave the order to file out. Myles Reilly and McDermott stayed at the windows. They were our two best riflemen. When we got to Donoghue's Cross the road was cut and trees knocked. We waited for Reilly and McDermott at the cross. Then we split up, half of us for the safe houses round the lakes and the rest of us headed into the mountains. We mightn't have bothered.'

'They were afraid to put their heads out and when they did they came in a whole convoy, shooting at women and children.'

'They were never the same again,' Moran said. 'News of it spread throughout the whole country.'

'You had a great head on you, Michael.'

'Only for you it couldn't have come to anything.'

17

'I remember clearer than yesterday his eyebrows. Not often you see an Englishman with red eyebrows. I had so much time to look at him I can hardly believe it still, pushing the trolley, standing up in Nibs's clothes. I had already loosened the overcoat and was thinking as I looked at him, This very minute you are going on the longest journey a man ever takes and you haven't a frigging clue. Then I fired.'

'I was watching you with the stopwatch.'

'We didn't have to split up that day. They were afraid of their shite to come out of the towns. The country was ours again. Next we had the Treaty. Then we fought one another.'

'Look where it brought us. Look at the country now. Run by a crowd of small-minded gangsters out for their own good. It was better if it never had happened.'

'I couldn't agree with that,' McQuaid said. 'The country is ours now anyhow. Maybe the next crowd will be better than this mixture of druids and crooks that we're stuck with.'

'Leave the priests out of it,' Moran said sharply.

'I'll leave nobody out of it. They all got on our backs.'

Moran did not answer. An angry brooding silence filled the room. McQuaid felt for the authority he had slowly made his own over the years, an authority that had outgrown Moran's. He would not move. Moran rose and went outside. McQuaid did not respond to him in any way when he came in again.

When Maggie returned she found them locked in the strained silence. Beforehand she had combed her hair by the light of the flashlamp, smoothed and rearranged her clothes but even if she hadn't Moran would not have noticed this evening. At once, in the silence, she began to make tea and sandwiches. Mona came down from upstairs and after whispering with Maggie disappeared again upstairs with a small jug of milk and some sandwiches. At last, out of the silence, Moran noticed McQuaid's glass was empty and attempted to pour him more whiskey.

'Cap it,' McQuaid said and covered his glass with his hand.

'There were years when you were able for most of the bottle.'

'Those years are gone. We'll have the tea Maggie is making.'

Reluctantly Moran screwed the cap back on the bottle and returned it behind the curtains of the medicine press. The tone in which *Cap it* had been said smarted like a cut.

'Do you remember Eddie McIniff in Maguire's garden on night watch?' McQuaid asked. 'He could see all the roads from Maguire's garden. We were watching in case the Tans would try to infiltrate the lakes at night. Eddie used to shoot a lot of duck and could stand like a stone. One of the Maguire girls – Ellie or Molly, I think it was Molly, they were all fine looking, tall women – came out to do her morning business and hunkered down under an apple tree a few feet away from Eddie. All Eddie did was to wait a bit and then lean over without a sound and lay the gun barrel across her back cheeks. I'd love to have seen her face when she jumped,' McQuaid laughed out loud. 'There must be nothing colder on a bare arse than a gun barrel that was out all night.'

Moran did not laugh. He looked helpless with the weight of his own disapproval. His two thumbs rotated about one another as they always did when he was agitated and looking for a way to strike.

'McIniff was blackguard enough to do that but you'd think that at least he'd be ashamed to tell it.'

'What was it but fun?' McQuaid brushed the criticism aside. 'Didn't·you have something to do with one of those Maguire girls? The rest of us had to scrape and scrounge for the girls, Michael, but whatever you had they always fell into your hands like ripe plums.'

'That was all talk,' Moran said, angry as ever at any baring of the inviolate secrecy he instinctively kept around himself.

'Your father was a hard man for the women in his day,' McQuaid said addressing the two girls.

'I think Mr McQuaid does himself less than credit with that talk,' Moran said with quiet dignity.

'There's even rumours that you're courting again. Are you thinking of taking the plunge, Michael?'

Moran held a pointed silence. The girls brought tea and sandwiches.

'Ah, these girls will make some man happy,' McQuaid said. 'But you're a brave man, Michael. If anything were to happen to my old dosey I'm afraid I'd live out my days in peace.'

The girls were able to laugh openly at last without any risk. The idea of the fat old cattle dealer emerging as a romantic possibility was so preposterous that even Moran smiled.

'I'd take that pension, Michael. You earned it. Take what they'll give you. Never question the colour of money.' The talk turned to easier waters as they drank tea.

'I've got on without it long enough. Why should I take it from them now?' It was plain from the blustering way he spoke that he wasn't so sure.

'It never did me no harm. There were times when I was starting in at the cattle that it stood between me and the road. It doesn't make much difference now but a hell of a sight of worse things come through the letterbox at the end of every month.'

'I was thinking of taking it,' Moran admitted.

'Wouldn't it buy something for the girls here or put someone through school even if you didn't want to take it for yourself? You should have taken it years ago. In this world you don't exist without money. And there might never be another world.' McQuaid could not resist this hit at Moran's religiosity.

'Man proposes . . .' Moran said darkly.

'And God stays out of it,' McQuaid twisted round the old saw.

The girls had washed and put away the cups and plates, covered the few squares of sandwiches that remained with a damp cloth. 'Mr McQuaid's room is ready,' Maggie said as they prepared to take their leave for the night. 'The bed is aired.'

'Oh, I forgot,' McQuaid said hastily. 'I have to be hitting the road any minute now. I should have told you earlier but it must have slipped the old mind.'

Moran did not protest. Covertly, leaning far back in his chair, he watched McQuaid from under hooded eyelids: in all the years they had been coming together on Monaghan Day McQuaid had always spent the night in the house.

'I told my old lady I'd be home,' McQuaid lied as he rose. 'Otherwise she'd have gone over to one of the boys. She gets afraid on her own in the house at night.'

Having waited long enough to see if they were needed, the two girls went up to Moran and kissed him on the lips as they did every night.

'Good night, Mr McQuaid,' they offered their hand.

'That was a great meal. Ye are a great pair of girls. If you ever get up our way call in to see my old lassie,' he took and held their hands.

'Good night, Mr McQuaid,' they repeated awkwardly before leaving the two men alone.

McQuaid sat down but almost immediately rose again. As on all the other Monaghan Days stretching far back he had come intending to stay the night. Tonight a growing irritation at Moran's compulsion to dominate, to have everything on his own terms or not at all, had hardened into a sudden decision to overturn the years and quit the house at once. As soon as Moran saw McQuaid on his feet again he knew the evening, all the evenings, were about to be broken up and he withdrew back into himself. He would neither plead with him to stay nor help him with his leaving.

As soon as McQuaid met Moran's domination of the evening with this sudden violence he was anxious to be conciliatory. 'Well, thanks for the meal and evening, Michael. It was a great evening.'

For a time it seemed that Moran might choose to remain seated and force McQuaid to make his own way out of the house. When he did rise in the chair it was slowly and grudgingly and he followed McQuaid out into the stone hallway as if he were finding it difficult to walk or move. He held his hand on the door's edge in the darkness of the hallway.

'Good luck, Michael,' the old cattle dealer said a last time but Moran made no answer in the darkness.

A brief moon between clouds outside sharpened the lines of boxwood that led to the wooden gate. McQuaid walked heavily and firmly to the gate. He did not bother to shut it, letting it swing open behind him. After opening the door of the Mercedes he leaned on its edge to clear his throat and spit on the yellow path.

'Some people just cannot bear to come in second,' he said loudly enough to be heard before getting into the car, reversing it round and driving away. Moran stood holding the edge of the door until the headlights disappeared and he closed the door without shutting the iron gate at the road or the small wooden gate leaning against the boxwood.

In a cold fury he stood and sat about for a long time within, twice changing from chair to chair. After years he had lost his oldest and best friend but in a way he had always despised friendship; families were what mattered, more particularly that larger version of himself – *his* family; and while seated in the same scheming fury he saw each individual member gradually slipping away out of his reach. Yes, they would eventually all go. He would be alone. That he could not stand. He saw with bitter lucidity that he would marry Rose Brady now. As with so many things, no sooner had he taken the idea to himself than he began to resent it passionately.

McQuaid had either struck true by pure chance or had picked up reliable gossip at the Mohill Fair.

Rose Brady had come home from Glasgow to nurse her father and stayed on irresolutely after his death, one day stretching into days. She could go back to the Rosenblooms, to the big house outside Glasgow where she had lived as one of the family for twelve years. Mrs Rosenbloom had written that they all wanted her back but still she stayed with her mother and brother in the farmhouse above the small lake, the poor rock-strewn lower slopes of the mountain rising towards Arigna beyond.

Sometimes in the evenings she had too strong a sense of being locked into the life of the farmhouse, even with the door continuously open on the summer yard, her brother away in the fields, her mother stumbling about the place with buckets, leaning on the table or the back of a chair whenever she stood to talk. One evening, as an excuse to get out of the house, she went with a letter to the post office.

To her surprise the small room of the post office was full of people waiting for the evening mail. They all turned towards her when she entered and way was made for her to go up to the counter. People whose own names she was no long certain of called out her name and she smiled and nodded by way of general response. The post office was owned by two white-haired sisters, Annie and Lizzie, far out cousins of her own, and Annie stamped the envelope for her, postmarked it and dropped it in the calico bag on the counter.

'You're still with us, Rose?'

'Still here, Annie. You've a big crowd this evening.'

'It's for the mail van. You might as well wait yourself to see if there's anything for the house.'

In turn she moved aside to allow someone else room at the counter and found herself standing beside Moran. She knew him well by sight but she had never spoken with him before.

'I was very sorry about your father,' he said.

'I know that,' she gave the formal response.

He had been a widower for many years, she knew. He had been an army officer once and there had been trouble that caused him to leave the army. Often she had passed the stone house where he lived with his children, some of whom must now be grown. She had heard dark mutterings about him but after a few minutes of talking with him she was ready to put it down to common envy. She found him attentive, intelligent, even charming, but with a distinct sense of separateness and pride that she found refreshingly unlike any of the other local men she had known. When the mail van pulled up outside, the hum of talk about them went silent. The driver dumped the mail bag on the counter, lifting the sealed bag without speaking a word. Annie opened the bag. As soon as she started to go through the bundle of letters, all Moran's attention was fixed on the sorting. He ignored Rose completely. From being the centre of his attention one moment all of a sudden she ceased to exist. His whole life seemed to hang on each letter in Annie's hand, his eyes following it until she handed it into the crowd or placed it on a pile to one side and then he would fix on the next letter and the next. The tension was such that she felt sudden relief as they went out of the small room into the air.

'Were you expecting an important letter?'

'No,' he laughed. 'What makes you think that?'

'Oh, I just wondered.'

'I come nearly every evening for the post. It gets you out of the place. It saves wondering the next day whether Jimmy Lynch will bring anything to the house or not.'

The bicycle she wheeled left thin tracks in the pale dust that covered the road. At the crossroads beside the bridge they parted.

'I suppose we'll be losing you again before too long,' he said.

'I'm not sure when I'll go back,' she answered.

She was in her late thirties, lean and strong, too neat and plain of feature ever to have been beautiful but her large grey eyes were intelligent and full of wilfulness and energy. As soon as she got home she couldn't resist bringing up Moran's name.

'They say he's no ornament,' her mother said carefully.

'I was talking to him in the post office.'

She saw her mother look at her sharply. 'They say he's one sort of person when he's out in the open among people – he can be very sweet – but that he's a different sort of person altogether behind the walls of his own house.'

'People talk too much about other people round here. Often the talk is just ignorant malice.'

Her true instinct was always to work behind the usual social frameworks: family, connections, position, conventions, those established forms that can be used like weapons when they are mastered. Behind them she could work with a charm and singleness of attention that became so smooth as to be chilling, except for the friendliness of her large grey eyes. The Rosenblooms had long known that they could take her with them anywhere in society. These skills she could not use with Moran.

Her interest was too great. She had too little time. There was too much of the outlaw about him that held its own fascination. Painfully and in the open she had to make all the running.

She came to the post office the next evening, and the next, buying tea and a comb of honey from Lizzie the first evening, posting a letter at Annie's counter on the Friday, waiting till the mail was sorted, each time managing to leave the post office alone with Moran. They stood talking a long time at the crossroads before separating but he didn't offer to see her over the weekend. She was able to conceal her restlessness, the pacing about, her dream of a different beginning to a new life, her impatience with the old shapes that she had used for too long; she was not young and was old enough to foresee failure. She was able to will her longing into an unexamined haze but she could not stay away from the post office on Monday. Once she appeared regularly others could observe her. Annie and Lizzie were friendly with Moran. They often discussed his family together and how hard it was for a single man to bring up children alone. Soon they began to greet Rose's evening presence in their small clean-scrubbed room with sarcasm. This unseemly chase after love was viewed with a hostile, overall amusement, for 'love' had left Annie and Lizzie – and many far younger – long behind and it was valued like jaundice. This courting dance seemed to them a grotesque parody.

Crossing the road to water the bed of dahlias and moon daisies and nasturtiums she kept on the grass margin across the road from her door at the beginning of the village, Mrs Reynolds paused to watch Rose make her way round by the bridge to the post office and muttered venomously, 'There's no fool like an old fool', as if confronting the worst part of her own nature. In the two bars, and on the bridge and football field where the men gathered in the evening, there were the coarse shouts of 'Sink log! All find their way to the dirty hollow', followed by cheers that echoed out like firing. In the full face of the ridicule she went to the post office evening after evening, ridicule she willed not to see or notice.

'Are you expecting some important letter, Rose?' her mother inquired anxiously.

'No, Mother. It just takes me out of the house for an hour or two.'

Then her married sister arrived at the house with news of her real reason for going each evening to the post office. 'You'd think she'd have more sense at her age. She'll just become a laughing stock if she's not that already.'

'I hear you're seeing Mr Moran at the post office,' her mother ventured delicately.

'Yes. He goes there every evening.'

'I wouldn't be too bothered about him. And besides he has a large family of his own already.'

'We're just friends, Mother,' she gave that little laugh and smiled the charming smile that hid the pure will. 'All we ever talk about is his children. He is very worried about them.'

'I'd be careful if I were you, Rose. It doesn't need much to start people talking.'

'Then let them talk.'

Yet Moran made no move towards her, promised nothing, gave no hint of any reciprocation of interest, lent her no support. All he did was remain at the point where they first met. He neither went towards her nor withdrew and she saw it could not go on like that. One evening as they were forced to shelter from a sudden shower under the thick line of sycamores, she said, 'You should call to the house some evening, Michael. I know they'd like to meet you.'

'You know how hard it is to get away, Rose.'

'Still, you know you're welcome,' she smiled and left him and he was not surprised when she did not come to the post office the next evening or the evening after. He knew that he would have to go to her if he wanted her.

As a young man he had been pursued by many women; that he secretly despised them did not lessen his attractiveness but in later years his large family and increasing years had hung about him with a weight as great as any deformity: but he would never risk exposing himself as Rose had. Rose Brady's

26

attention had been as unexpected as it had been sudden and welcome. It was as if she had fallen out of a generous sky. She was much younger than he, strong, not unpleasant to look at. He had reason to suspect that she had saved money and his life could glow again in the concentration of her attention. It was unlikely that such luck would fall his way again no matter how long he waited. That same week he told Maggie out of the blue that he wanted to see her alone. With great nervousness and alarm she followed him to his room.

'There's something very important that concerns all the family that I want to discuss seriously.' He felt garbed in the robes of responsibility and consequence as he spoke. 'What would you think if I were to bring someone new into the family?'

Maggie looked quickly at him but without comprehension.

'If I was to fill your mother's place – the Lord have mercy on her soul – with someone new,' he amended. 'If I were to marry again.'

Whether it was the sudden mention of her mother or the whole emotional portentousness with which he had charged the scene Maggie burst out sobbing. This continued for a long time during which he shuffled his feet uncomfortably, controlling his immediate impulse to shout at her to be quiet. After a while she discovered that she could hide comfortably behind the shelter of sobbing.

'A woman would be able to help you in ways that I can't,' he said. 'There's only so much any man can do on his own.'

'Whatever you think, Daddy.' She knew that whatever she said would be irrelevant anyhow.

'You think it would be for the best then?' He was impatient now to conclude the whole scene.

'If you think it's for the best, Daddy.'

'I know it'll be for the best. I wouldn't even think of it for a minute if it wasn't best for everybody. After all these years it'll be a real house and home again. It'll be a place that will always be there for you to come back to.'

She could not wait to tell Sheila and Mona. Both girls thought she was joking at first but when she recounted word for word the interview she had had with Moran they exploded into wild laughter. They did not tell their younger brother. Though they loved him as if he were their own child they left him out of all things that mattered in the running of the house.

'Who is she?' They asked when they were quiet again.

'It must be Miss Brady that's home from Glasgow.'

'She'd never have him.'

'They say she's wild after him. She goes every evening to the post,' and they began to laugh again at what they saw as a mocking mirror of their own flowering.

Moran took the small blue Ford out of the shed after Mass on Sunday, tested the engine and tyres, then washed the car down, dried it and waxed it till it shone. At three o'clock he drove the four miles to Rose Brady's house. The lane into the house was narrow and winding with too many gates so he parked the car on the wide grass margin beside the platform for the creamery cans. The car could not be seen from the house because of the shelter of trees. He walked slowly down the lane, enjoying the feel of the pressed brown suit he so seldom wore, this new excitement midst the humdrum of his life. It was as if he were going to the edge again of something fresh and new.

Rose saw him at the heavy red gate of the yard. So intense was her relief at seeing him come that she stood stock-still in the doorway. As relief spread to pure pleasure she waved and came towards him across the yard like a young girl. She was already by his side before she thought of how her face and hair must look.

She had gone through bad days. In the evenings, with painful vividness, she had seen the small congregation in the post office, the mail van crossing the bridge, Annie sorting the letters, the stretch of empty road to the sycamores where they had stopped to talk. Such was the restlessness of her longing to go there that she had had to struggle to stick to her resolve. She could not go. She had given signs enough, perhaps too many, and she could only wait. Now he had come to her.

Though her mother disliked him the custom of hospitality

28

was too strict to allow any self-expression or unpleasantness. Her brother he had met before and the two men talked about the year's haysaving and the price they expected for sheep and wool and cattle. A white cloth was spread on the table, home-made bread and jam, a fresh apple tart. Tea was made. He praised the bread and the blackcurrant jam.

'The garden is choked every year with blackcurrants. The birds get most of them. Your girls should come here to pick them next summer.'

'That would be too much,' he said.

'If the girls don't pick them they'll just waste in the grass or go with the birds,' the mother said as amiably as she could.

'Are you interested in football?' her brother asked.

'Not so much but it's nice to see a good match.'

'Would you like to hear the end of the game then?'

'Sure I would,' and her brother turned on the Sunday game he had been listening to when Moran entered the yard. After ten minutes or so it seemed to end satisfactorily. Moran was unassertive and attentive in the few minutes they discussed the game afterwards.

'Now that I've eaten and drunk my fill it's time for me to beat away,' he said after about an hour.

Rose's mother and brother shook his hand politely. She got a cardigan and walked him all the way out the lane. Above them rose the poor fields, littered with rock and gorse, the lower slopes of the mountain. Below the lane was the small lake ringed with reeds.

'Are there fish in the lake?'

'There used to be plenty – small perch, and pike, and eel – but they never seemed to grow to any size.'

When they went through the first gate at the bottom of the hill they were out of people's eyes for the first time since they had met. There were just the whitehorn and brier of the hedges, the green ridge of the lane inside the wheel tracks, the wild strawberries starting to darken on the banks.

'Was I all right in the house?' he asked.

'You were perfect. You could not have been better. It was

lovely that you came,' and she took his hand and raised her mouth eagerly to his as he bent to kiss her for the first time.

'I'm not used to going out,' he said. 'You'll have to come to meet my crowd now.'

'I'd love to meet them.'

'One of these evenings I'll arrange it. I hope they'll know how to show manners.' Responsibility visibly descended on him again as he walked.

'I didn't know you had a car,' she said with surprise when they reached the road.

'I don't take it out very often but it's nice to have, to know that you can go anywhere you want if you feel like it.'

Secretly she exulted that he had the car. It was just one more sign of his separateness from the people around who would buy a cow or a few more fields. In these parts a car was prized more than flowers or an orchard or a herb garden: it was the symbol of pure luxury.

She walked slowly back down the lane, savouring the rich peace, the strength she felt. This narrow lane was dear to her. Sleepless in Scotland she had walked it many times in her mind. The wild strawberries, the wiry grasses, the black fruit of the vetches on the banks were all dear presences. Out of the many false starts her life had made she felt they were witnessing this pure beginning that she would seize and make true. No longer, exposed and vulnerable, would she have to chase and harry after happiness. From a given and confident position she would now be able to move outwards.

'Where's Tom?' she noticed her brother's absence as soon as she got back to the house.

'He said he was going over to O'Neill's for an hour.'

'I didn't meet him on the lane.'

'He must have just gone over the fields.'

After a long silence the mother said, 'That was a bit of a surprise visit.'

'I asked him to call if he was ever this way. Did you like him at all?'

'If he suits you I'm sure he suits me. He has a large family.'

'I don't see how that can be held against him.'

'You used to have many admirers,' the mother changed.

'The admirers are all gone.' Both women were glad to let the conversation drop. They would not change.

She did not go to the post office the next evening or the next. No longer had she the ache of longing for that stretch of white road leading round to the sycamores. By coming to the house on Sunday Moran had made that stretch of road like all roads. She would go on the day she judged best. She did not want to appear either too eager or too casual.

All her nervousness came back as she approached the post office just ahead of the mail van. The small room was full. Moran was there and smiled on her and spoke. Whether Annie and Lizzie had heard of the Sunday visit or had marked her absence wasn't clear but they appeared almost conciliatory compared to previous days. She did notice too that Moran was more carelessly dressed than she remembered and hadn't shaved for at least a day. It was as if he were truculently stating that he had gone as far towards her as he was prepared to go. Outside the post office he made no apology for the roughness of his appearance but he was as friendly and charming as he had always been.

'There's a concert in the hall on Sunday. It'd be easier if we met my troops for the first time at the concert,' he said. 'Then you can come to the house any time you want to afterwards.'

'Whatever you think is best.' She was glad to do whatever he wished.

On Saturday night at the end of the Rosary Moran said, 'I want to offer a final prayer to God that He may guide your father on the right course,' and they all knew, even to the boy Michael, to what he was referring. 'There's a very special person I want you to meet at the concert tomorrow. I hope you'll all like her. She's Miss Brady,' he told them as soon as they rose from their knees. They made vague general noises about how glad they would be to meet her. 'I want everybody dressed in their best clothes,' Moran demanded.

Sunday evening the girls were shining and the boy wore his

blue Confirmation suit with black shoes. They were all excited and a little ashamed. They had seen Miss Brady in the distance at Mass but they had never met her. At the hill beyond the village he gave them money. 'Go up to the front row and keep two chairs,' he directed and then left them. Though the hall was almost empty they weren't forward enough to go into the very front seats so they entered the seats three rows back, claiming two extra chairs with folded coats. They knew all the people entering the hall, and those that occupied seats close to them smiled and spoke to them. They felt nervous and compromised. They were even more uncomfortable when their father entered with Rose just as the full hall was waiting for the curtain to go up. With extreme slowness Moran walked Rose to the seats. The girls suffered agonies of exposure as they waited for them to reach their seats. Slowly and solemnly Moran introduced Rose to each member of the family in turn. The small group became more the centre of attention than the stage itself. Rose's tact was never more evident. If she was nervous it remained hidden and in a few minutes she had put each of the sisters completely at ease, their shame and apprehension gone.

The concert was amateur. A group of girls decked with medals danced. A blue-suited man sang. An old man played several airs on an accordion. The drama society put on a short comic sketch. As all the performers were either related to or known to the audience each act was greeted with loud and equal applause. At the interval Rose nodded and smiled to the people about her. Moran made no gesture, did not even look around him.

At the end of the concert he took the four children back to Great Meadow. Rose sat in the front seat. At the house he invited Rose in but she refused with the excuse that it was too late. As she said goodnight to them in turn she managed by some technique of charm or pure personality to convey to each of them that they were important to her in their own light. They left her feeling completely enclosed in a warm glow of attention and to Moran's repeated questions over the next days were able to say genuinely how much they liked her. In fact, the response was so uniform and repetitious that it started to irritate him before long.

Rose wished that they could be married quickly but now that there was nothing in the way of it Moran grew cautious and evasive. She saw the way it was and moved differently. An invitation through Moran brought the three girls and the boy to her house for a long Sunday. As it came through Rose he encouraged it as much as he would have discouraged visits to any other neighbouring house.

She showed them the small lake in its ring of reeds, took them to the first slopes of the mountain, rigged up a fishing rod for Michael and took him to the part of the lake she used to fish as a girl, and soon he was shouting out in glee as he missed the ravenous little perch or swung them out over his head on to the bank. Rose's mother showed the girls the house and the fowl and farm animals, including a pet goat who wouldn't let Rose milk her unless she sprayed herself with a perfume that the mother used. They were given a sumptuous tea and invited back any time they felt like coming. Within a few weeks they were regular visitors. As Moran encouraged them they could go without guilt. To leave the ever-present tension of Great Meadow was like shedding stiff, formal clothes or kicking off pinching shoes. Old Mrs Brady never took to Moran but she grew very fond of the children. Until she won their trust their manners were deferential, identical to the old-fashioned manners of her own youth. They were always eager to help or run messages and she enjoyed making tea and cakes for them. Rose, with the same tact as she had brought them to the house, was careful to absent herself from these occasions as much as possible. She sent them alone with sandwiches and drinks to where her brother worked in the fields and he too grew glad of their quiet company in the empty fields. In a few months Rose's home place and Moran's house were almost interwoven. Half-jokingly, but with a certain edge, Moran said that Great Meadow was so deserted that he himself might have to remove himself before long to her house. No one was ever able to see quite how it had all been managed. Rose's tact was so masterful that she resembled certain people who are so deeply read that they can play with all ideas without ever listing books.

'What do you think of Rose marrying your father?' the old woman grew confident enough one day to ask Maggie in her good-humoured, forceful way.

'We're glad.'

'Are you sure you don't mind?'

'No, we're glad.'

'People say he used beat ye.'

'People said that because Daddy never let us mix with them.'

'Did he not beat ye?'

'No . . . now and again when we were bold, but like any house.' Shame as much as love prompted the denial.

'How is it that your brother left and never came home?'

'Daddy and Luke could never get on. They were too alike,' and when Maggie began to cry Rose's mother saw that she had pressed too hard.

'She'd have been better with someone nearer her own age,' the old woman murmured to herself. 'She had many admirers. Many admirers. Many admirers. I don't understand it at all.'

Maggie brushed away her tears as she listened. She thought the mutterings were comical. To her both Rose and Moran looked equally old. Rose's mother was not reassured by Maggie's answers but she liked her and didn't want to endanger their young presences about the house.

Michael had become her favourite. He was the least inhibited. He would chatter away egotistically to her for hours. Sometimes she would give him money on the sly and he would help her with chores. Often they would quarrel and he would stay away from the house for a while; but he was never able to stay away for long. When he would return, the two would feel even closer than before the quarrel and they would soon be moving about the yard together, chatting away.

For all her encouragement to them to come at any time to her house, Rose herself was wary of calling at Great Meadow.

Whenever she did she never stayed for long. When Moran pressed her to come for the Christmas dinner, she refused. 'It wouldn't look right to be out of my own house on Christmas Day,' she answered; that they were not yet married was left unsaid. 'I'll come some time early on St Stephen's Day,' she said instead.

The girls wished that Rose could be with them on Christmas Day. As always, it was a very long day to get through. Moran ate alone in front of the big sideboard mirror, waited on apprehensively by the girls. After he had eaten, they had their own dinner at the side table. It was the first Christmas anybody had even been absent and Moran seemed to be painfully aware of Luke's absence.

'You'd think he'd come for the Christmas or even write but never a word, no thought for anybody except himself,' and it cast a deep shadow when they tried to imagine what kind of space enclosed Luke in England during the same hour, but they weren't able to imagine it. It was too much like facing darkness. Afterwards the radio was played. The Rosary was said. The pack of cards was taken out. Everybody made for their beds early. It was a gladness to slip down into the sheets knowing the day had ended.

The next morning Rose came in with presents. She had bought a silk tie for Moran, blouses and deep plum-coloured sweaters for the girls, a pair of white football boots for Michael. Because of his dislike of gifts, the girls watched carefully how Moran would receive the silk tie.

'Thanks, Rose,' he said and placed it on top of the radio.

'Don't you like it?' She smiled a little, taken aback by the spareness of the response.

'It cost far too much and is far too grand for an old fellow like me.' The response was positively exuberant.

Just as Rose was preparing to leave, the wren-boys arrived on the Arigna coal lorry. There must have been twenty men on the back of the lorry in masks and carnival costumes. With the money they gathered from different houses, they bought ham, loaves and butter, lemonade, whiskey and half-barrels of porter to hold a big dance in Kirkwood's barn that night. Everyone around was invited.

As soon as they came into the house a melodeon started to play and two fiddles took up in perfect tune; then bagpipes played alone. Young men danced Rose Brady and the girls round the kitchen. There were whoops and cheers, mock kissing attempts, challenges to put names on the masked faces and then a song.

'The two of you will have to come to the Major's tonight,' the man who gathered the money said.

'Maybe we will,' Moran responded. 'Maybe we will.'

Moran gave them a pound, Rose took a red ten-shilling note from her handbag and they left in the same whirl as they had entered, dancing and singing all the way out to the lorry. An eerie silence descended over the house as the lorry left for the next house.

'Are we going to the dance?' Rose asked Moran as she left.

'What would be seen there but the same old crowd making fools of themselves?'

'It's Christmas.'

'Do you want to go?'

'I'd like to very much.'

He went reluctantly. There was an air of great jollity and freedom, even of outright licence, at the wren-boys' dance in Kirkwood's barn. Moran didn't feel easy. The air of friendliness was the kind that he disliked most. The wren-boys who had gone from house to house on the lorry all day were now scrubbed and combed, playing away cheerfully on raised planks. Even though there was a sharp frost outside, couples could be seen stealing away from the dance and returning a half-hour or so later, always a little crestfallen until they had danced again, danced their way back into good cheer. Moran hardly spoke to anybody and reacted roughly to any jostling as he danced with Rose on the warped floor. Rose was anxious, feeling that he had lived in the stone house with too much responsibility for too long. He had not been able to go out and be at ease with people. What she did not know was that Moran, with his good looks and military fame, had once been king of these barn dances and now that he had neither youth nor fame would not take a lesser place. He would not take part at all.

Rose had come to the dance to claim their place as a couple among the people in this loose, Christmas carnival. She was determined to remain. She smiled and chatted with everybody around her. She took tea. She danced with neighbours and men she had gone to school with. She forced Moran to dance and by the night's end she was worn out by the single effort. He had given her no help throughout the night but it did not lessen her love.

In the car, leaning her head on his consenting but exasperated shoulder, she said, 'We don't have to be like the rest of the people round here. We don't have to go out together for years. There's nothing in the way of our getting married, and I love you, Michael.'

'When do you want to get married?'

'This year. Before the summer. If there was something in our way it would be different.'

'There's the children to consider.'

'I'd not be in the way of the children. I could only be of help.'

'When do you want to be married then?'

'We have nothing to stop us before Lent.'

'It'd be too rushed,' he said. 'It'll have to be after Lent.'

'The week after Easter then.' She set the time and was too happy to notice that he was more like a man listening to a door close than one going towards his joy.

'We'll have the wedding breakfast in the Royal. There won't be need to invite many,' she proposed carefully some days later.

'I don't want anything in an hotel.'

'We have to have some place for a reception,' she argued.

'Haven't we two houses of our own?'

'I don't think they'd like that at home. As soon as I mentioned an Easter wedding they brought up the Royal.'

'The Bradys don't have that much money to scatter at the Royal Hotel.'

'They don't mind that. It's just one day.'

'There'll be no hotels. We are too old and poor for that.'

'It'll be thought strange. Everybody does it.'

'Because everybody goes and jumps in the river is no reason why we have to go and jump in the same river.'

'I know that what you say makes sense, love,' she placed her hand on his arm. 'They'll not like it at home. They'll not understand. Can't we go to the Royal for them?'

'Let them start to understand,' he said as he took her hand in a playful threat. 'We can always have ham and tea and whiskey for anybody that wants it in our house. That way we'll have less travelling to do afterwards.'

As a play it was close to perfect. The honour of the reception always fell to the family of the bride. It would not do for it to take place in Moran's house and Moran would not go to a hotel. The Bradys would have to agree to hold it in their house or not at all.

Eventually Rose persuaded them to hold the reception in the house. They did not like it, argued against it – argued against the whole match – but she held firm. There would be fewer people to cope with that way, and she wasn't young any longer.

The night before the wedding the girls hardly slept at all and they did not chatter to one another as they usually did until they found sleep. In the morning their father would be married. Another woman would come back with him into the house. It did not matter that it was the Rose they had grown to like. The life they had come to know so well for so long as it slipped by changelessly would be irrevocably altered: it was like a death or a wounding and brought all the wonder and fear and awe of change. Each of their own lives would have to take up another uncertain beginning.

Moran himself slept fitfully beside their brother. Now and again he would reach a hand over to the boy but he slept deeply through the night. It would be his last night of sleep in the room. The small boxroom with a single bed was already prepared. Tomorrow night Rose would lie in the boy's place. When he did wake, Moran reached his hand across to the coarse shirt over the shoulder and gently began to knead the muscles.

'It's the last time we'll wake in the morning together.'

'The last time,' the boy repeated uncertainly.

'You know what day it is?'

'Your wedding day.'

'It's the end of one life. The beginning of a different life. I believe it's in the best interest of all the family. We can only pray and hope it'll turn out for the best.'

The boy was always more uncomfortable with these essays in tenderness than any sudden harshness. He sat up immediately in the bed to listen.

'They're up,' he announced. 'They're all up. Do you want me to draw the curtain, Daddy?'

'No. Not yet,' Moran said but the boy had already drawn free from the kneading hand and was struggling into his clothes. He closed the door softly behind him and was gone without another word. Moran lay on in bed till very late. One of the girls had to come to the door to call him.

'Your clothes is aired and ready, Daddy. It's time to get up.'

He came in in his old trousers and nightshirt. They were already dressed for the wedding, wearing little bits of borrowed fineries they were afraid he would notice. The boy was wearing his blue suit, shining black shoes, white shirt and blue tie and his fair hair was oiled. The kettle was boiling and Maggie poured the water into the basin in front of the shaving mirror. He failed to notice the borrowed things that the girls wore, looking around him instead in dumb bafflement: it was a wedding day, a shining moment in his life, and, except for the dressed children, it could be any ordinary day. His clothes were draped on the back of a chair in front of the fire. The clothes horse was drawn up. The steaming water was waiting in the basin before the mirror. He felt a low cry of frustration against the inadequacy of life break silently within, and ripple out. 'What time is it?' he demanded fiercely.

'It's just ten, Daddy. There's only an hour till the Mass.'

'I think I know it takes an hour to get from ten to eleven.' The sarcasm seemed to relieve him a little and he took the black strop of leather from its nail and opened the razor. The blade flashed as it was drawn over the leather. He lathered and started to shave. They all fixed in a pure tenseness of watching as he shaved but he did not cut himself. He washed and towelled himself dry. 'Your uncle didn't put in an appearance yet?'

'No, there's no sign of him.'

When he started to dress in front of the fire the two older girls turned away and when he looked for a collar stud the boy ran to attend. Once Maggie caught a glimpse of him in the shaving mirror, trouserless but with his shirt and socks on and in spite of her fear she was tempted to laugh. Trouserless men looked absurd in socks. He dressed with great care. He had refused to buy any new clothes for the wedding but the brown suit had been brushed and pressed. The white shirt was starched and the shoes shone. He went back to the shaving mirror to comb his hair and when he had finished he pushed a folded handkerchief into his sleeve with quiet satisfaction.

'Of course, that uncle of yours didn't have the manners to write, never mind the decency to come; but I've long learned never to expect anything from an ass but a kick.' The increasing nervousness showed in his voice. 'I don't know why people can't write a note.'

They were all dressed. There was nothing to do but wait for their uncle. Moran had decided that they would go to the church in their uncle's big old car. They hadn't seen him in months. Moran had written to him and assumed that he would come. Several times Moran went to the front door to look towards the road. He changed his handkerchief from his left sleeve to his right.

'I should have learned by now never to rely on anybody.'

'He must have got a puncture,' Michael offered.

'You'd think he'd allow for that on a day the like of this.'

'He might never have thought . . .'

'You can rely on that. The man's head was designed to keep his ears apart. Anyhow we can't wait much longer.'

He went out and started the small blue Ford, backed it out of the shed and left the engine running.

'We better be going. We can't wait about like this any longer. God, O God, did you ever see such people!' They all crammed into the car. 'You'd think people would have heed, but no heed, never any heed, no care for anybody else,' he complained as he drove; but before the bridge he startled them by driving the car into the space in front of McCabe's and announcing that they would walk the rest of the way through the village.

'We're early. This way we'll meet the man on his bloody way if he's coming.'

Michael sniggered behind Moran as soon as they were on the road together but it drew such a quelling look from Maggie that he went quiet. All the girls were deeply ashamed. No one had ever seen a bride or groom walk to their wedding; even the very poor found a car for that day and in the old days they had gone by trap or sidecar. Fortunately the bridge was empty as was the long road of sycamores to the church in its dark evergreens. After crossing the bridge Moran checked his watch and to their infinite relief started to walk quickly. They wished their uncle would come and they could vanish into the huge car but no motor could be heard in the direction from which he would come. They walked on in silence. It had not rained for a week and the white dust of the road started to dull the shine of all the shoes. At the end of the long road Reynolds' was the first house they had to pass and they started to cringe into themselves behind Moran even before they got to the little hedge of privet above the whitewashed stones. Mrs Reynolds was in the doorway, almost ready herself to go to the wedding – she never missed a wedding or a funeral – but seeing the procession that approached withdrew back into the shadows of the room to observe better the old cockerel go by followed by his dismayed pullets.

'And the bloody madman is walking to his own wedding with all the children,' she said, more in sympathy with the children than in laughter.

Each step seemed to take an age as they passed the forge.

41

Only the boy looked at the two men sledging a length of iron on the outside anvil. Then they had to brace themselves to pass the few people standing along the church wall. None of them looked up as they passed. Moran did not turn to speak. There were curious villagers waiting for the wedding to begin in the back seats of the church but they did not look to left or right. All the children blessed themselves from the fount and went straight up to the altar. It was like the beginning of healing to get into their seats and kneel beside Moran, no longer exposed. None of the bride's party had come yet. The priest came through the sacristy door in soutane and surplice and Moran went up to the rails.

'The best man hasn't come. Would the boy do?' Moran asked. They both looked towards Michael.

'He's a bit young,' the priest said. 'We can get one of the bride's brothers to stand in.'

Then a car was heard pulling up at the gate; either the bridal car or their uncle had come. All turned to look back at the door as the footsteps approached on the flagstones. The relief showed instantly on their faces as the small round figure of their uncle filled the doorway. He hurried up the aisle of the church, showing his palms by way of apology when he reached his place. There were dirt and grease stains on both palms with bits of grass stuck to the grease.

'I thought you'd never get here,' Moran said.

'I got broke down,' he whispered apologetically as he slipped in beside Moran, putting his oily hand on the head of one of the girls. From the altar the priest nodded a smile of recognition to the best man. Finally Rose's family filed into the pew across the aisle and Rose came behind on her brother's arm. There was no music. The priest beckoned Moran forward. He motioned to them when to kneel, to stand, to be seated, when to take the ring, the gold and silver, to 'repeat these words after me'. A sister of Rose's sobbed briefly. The girls' eyes filled with tears. A man in the side-chapel took photos. The bride and groom returned together to the front seat for the nuptial Mass. Everybody except the best man went to the rails for Holy Com-

42

munion. Outside, in the clear day, as the couple stood beneath the bell rope, a small box of confetti was thrown. They stood together, separately, and then in groups for photos that one of Rose's sisters took, headstones and evergreens rising out of the background of thick laurel. The uncle's car was an old Ford V8 with enormous fins and there was more than enough room for all of them in the back. The bride and bridegroom rode in front.

'You gave us all a start,' Rose said happily. 'For a few minutes our hearts were in our mouths. We thought you weren't coming but it's wonderful you got here.'

'I got this puncture. She just went flat,' he turned his grease-stained hands upwards again on the wheel as he drove.

'You'll have hot water for them as soon as we get to the house.'

'You must have left it very tight to get here so late,' Moran said.

'You never think you'll get anything.'

'Of course nobody ever thinks. That goes without saying.'

'Everything is fine now. Their uncle got here and that is all that matters,' Rose smoothed, turning to chat to the girls in the back.

The car was too large for the lane so they walked in. The April Saturday was mild, with just the faintest threat of showers. Everywhere in the low briers and hedgerows was the clatter and singing of small birds. The little lake below the house was still ringed with its winter reeds, the colour of rained-on wheat. Everybody waited to eat until the priest arrived. He was the only one to risk his small car on the lane. He would have to leave early on a sick call, he said.

There were no letters or telegrams to be read out. The priest, with folded hands and closed eyes, recited Grace, and the meal began: soup served by a daughter of the same sister of Rose's who had been taking the photos; chicken and ham, with salad. The wedding cake was cut. The priest made a short speech praising the families and the outstanding simplicity of the wedding feast. There was too much emphasis nowadays on show, on Rolls-Royces and big hotels, wasteful, expensive display. It was pleasant to see people returning to the old ways, he said. There was wine and whiskey and beer for the toast. The best man said he wasn't used to speeches, he nearly hadn't arrived at all himself, but he just wanted to thank Father here for all he had done and the people of the bride here for this feast and all the trouble they had gone to, and then he proposed the toast. The brother who had given Rose away responded even more briefly and soon afterwards the priest left.

Gradually the wedding breakfast was breaking up. One of Rose's tall silent brothers went around the tables with a bottle of wine and a bottle of whiskey but they drank sparingly. When the best man cleared his throat and announced that he was going to fix the puncture he had before leaving, all Moran's children followed him out to the road and stood around as he got levers and patches and solution. When he came back to the house he refused to take a chair or a drink.

'I better be making a start. I have a run to do yet this evening.'

'We might as well go with you so,' Moran said and Rose got up eagerly. She had all her going-away things packed. The remaining things she could come back for any day. Her mother and sisters and brothers all embraced her but she showed no emotion. The whole household walked them out to the big Ford at the end of the lane. They embraced Rose a second time and everybody shook hands. At the bridge Moran and Rose changed to their own small blue car and the uncle drove the children home. He waited at the house until the bride and groom arrived but he could not be persuaded to enter the house.

The whole of Rose's family walked back down the lane to their house in silence. 'She had many admirers,' the old mother said as they neared the house in a tone of puzzlement and of mourning. 'Many admirers . . . Many admirers . . .'

'Nothing could stop her. She was determined on it. Now it's her life,' her married sister said gently.

'I hope she'll be lucky,' the wife of one of the brothers said without any feeling.

The four tall brothers walked in stooped silence but their

wives chatted agreeably. A daughter held the mother's hand in sympathy.

When they entered the house one of the brothers reached for the bottle of whiskey and poured four large glasses for the first time that day. They were a very close family but in the years to come no gathering or wedding, not even simple gatherings, was ever held in any one of their houses. They went to big hotels as if determined never again to experience anything like this house wedding in all their mortal lives. Neither Rose nor Moran ever attended any of the gatherings. They were never invited. They would not have gone if they were.

'I don't know about anybody else but I'd love a nice hot cup of tea,' Rose said as soon as they were all in the house. At once she set a tone that would not be easily wrested from her. Moran watched in silence.

All the girls helped her to get the fire going, spread the tablecloth, put out the cups and plates, laughing and whispering and bustling about as they showed her the places and secrets of the kitchen, the room that was now her room. There was a touch of hysteria in the frantic busyness. Their exaggeration of the small tasks betrayed that they were more involved with Moran than in what they were doing. Sometimes they would accidentally bring it to crisis by letting a plate or cup smash on the floor. As they showed her the house, Rose seemed to enter completely into the terrible awareness of Moran now sitting in the car chair meditatively rotating his thumbs about one another. On this his wedding day he seemed strangely at peace. It was as if he needed this quality of attention to be fixed upon him in order to be completely silent.

During the entire day he felt a violent, dissatisfied feeling that his whole life was taking place in front of his eyes without anything at all taking place. Distances were walked. Words were said. Rings were exchanged. The party moved from church to house. All seemed a kind of mockery. It was as if nothing at all had happened. He was tired of wrestling with it, brooding about it, sometimes looking at his bride's back with violent puzzlement; but now, surrounded by this covert attention, he was glad to let it go: he would take tea like a lord with his family.

Was there milk enough or a little too much in his tea? They could add more tea once he had taken a few sips. He didn't take sugar any more. Would he have the plain bread or the bread with the blackcurrant jam or a piece of the apple tart? 'The tea was all right,' he protested and they knew he was far from displeased. 'It'll do for the man it is for. I've already eaten enough today to do a man for a week. I'd explode if I was to put as much as one morsel more in my mouth.'

Rose and the girls smiled as the tea and the plates circled around him. They were already conspirators. They were mastered and yet they were controlling together what they were mastered by.

'Thanks,' he put his cup away. 'I'll go out to the fields for a few hours to try to work off some of this.'

He changed into his old clothes and left. They washed and dried the cups and plates and put them away. A quiet that was close to let-down replaced the wild bustle of the preparation but they were enjoying each other's company, the animal comfort of other presences, banishment of loneliness.

Outside, Moran thinned several small ash trees from the hedge that ran along the foot of the orchard. He liked mechanical things and he was pleased that the chainsaw he had had to dismantle several times in the past seemed to run perfectly. 'It must have been the timing that was out all along.' The felling, trimming, cutting, absorbed him completely and because of the ferocity of the running chain it demanded his undivided attention. Michael followed him out and helped pile the waste branches into heaps for burning and then they stacked the scattered lengths of the firewood.

Inside, the girls showed Rose all over the house. After that she began to tell them a little about her life in Scotland, particularly her life with the Rosenblooms.

'Sometimes at the weekend Mr Rosenbloom would come and

46

ask me to iron his shirts. He had hundreds of shirts and why he ever wanted *me* to iron them I'll never know. Mrs Rosenbloom nearly always found out about it and she would be mad that he had taken me from my work with the children. There'd be a battle royal all morning. After lunch he'd go into the city and come back with a whole armful of roses, the price of many shirts.'

'Would she be satisfied with that?' the girls demanded greedily.

'She'd hold out for a while but it would always be made up after he came back with the roses. He'd swear of course that he'd never again steal me from my proper duties with the children. She'd cut and arrange the roses. They'd dress up then and go out to dinner to some restaurant, laughing and talking together as if nothing at all had happened.'

'What would they be talking about, Rose?'

'About what they'd eat that evening in the restaurant and what wines they'd drink. You would wonder how they could eat at all after the amount of time they spent talking about food.'

When Moran came in from the field with Michael he was in high good humour.

'This man and me are after slaughtering a few trees out there.'

Even the way he hung his hat was expansive, drawing the whole room in. The girls knew how soon this mood could change if it was not fully entered into.

'I'm fit to tackle a live child again,' he joked as they prepared to eat.

'Now Michael, that's hardly necessary,' Rose scolded gently.

'It might not be but it's the godalmighty truth,' he asserted so playfully back that the whole table laughed.

After the tea he suggested that they play cards, already shuffling the cards he took from the sill. They played Twenty-one; the scores were kept on the inside of a Lyons Green Label tea packet. Moran was the best player and mostly won but that night he attributed his winnings to the cards he had been dealt. They knelt to the Rosary. Moran began, 'Thou, O Lord, wilt

47

open my lips,' as he began every evening. There was a pause when he ended the First Mystery. All their eyes were turned on Rose but she, with just a glance at Moran, took up the Second Mystery as if she had been saying it with them all the nights of their lives.

After the prayers they went up in turn and kissed Moran and then Rose who returned their kisses warmly, and they slipped away to their rooms. The boy was going to the boxroom and was clearly excited at possessing a room of his own for the first time. He too kissed Rose. Rose and Moran sat on alone in the room. They were not silent but only spoke after long intervals and what they said did not carry to the upstairs rooms. When the couple did go to their bedroom the girls became even more wide awake than before. They tried not to breathe as they listened. They were too nervous and frightened of life to react to or put into words the sounds they heard from the room where their father was sleeping with Rose.

Rose was up at seven the next morning, an hour before the house usually stirred. When the girls came down they found the room already warm, the fire lit, the kettle steaming. Rose was preparing to bring Moran a mug of tea.

'Daddy wouldn't hear of having his breakfast in bed,' she said with a small engaging laugh. 'But he might as well have this before getting up.'

She made an enormous difference in the house. Since their mother's death it had been run by Maggie, with bits of help from Mona and Sheila. At first their mother's sister had come from time to time but she and Moran had quarrelled. He was not interested in food other than it should not cost too much and wasn't raw. The girls had never been taught to cook or housekeep. They could cook vegetables and meat simply, deal with eggs and bacon and porridge, and they were able to bake and housekeep, learning as they went along. They didn't need to know much more.

Rose changed everything. She was able to organize her day so that even though she seemed to be less harassed than Maggie the meals were always delicious and on time. Then she began to clean and paint the house room by room. Moran complained about the unnecessary disturbance though it was the cost that he was secretly worried by. She pointed out that the plaster would soon fall away without paint. Whenever he complained too much about cost she went and bought what she needed with her own money. That he disliked even more. In the end he always gave what she asked but he resented the giving. She did not seem to mind and she was inordinately careful. 'You know Daddy,' she would laugh defensively with the girls. All the children helped her redecorate the house. When it was done the whole house had acquired a new pleasantness and comfort. Even Moran had to admit it though he dismissed it as well by saying that it would have done well enough for the likes of him as it had been.

What was also clear was that the house's need of Maggie had disappeared. Rose brought this up very gently to Moran.

'She'll have a roof over her head as long as I'm above ground,' he responded aggressively.

'She'll have that as long as I'm here too but I think she should have more.'

'What more does she want?'

'She's almost nineteen. The day is gone when a girl waits around till some man needs a wife. She should have the protection of some work.'

'What job of any good would she get here? She left school at fourteen. She wasn't all that good at school either.'

'There's a shortage of nurses in England. I always regretted I never trained. I've spoken to her and she's interested.'

'You were very quick off the mark, weren't you? A lot of our people go wrong in England.'

'I was there for a while,' she said pointedly but she was careful not to press too much. She had heard already from the girls how Luke had tried to get Maggie to go to England to learn nursing against Moran's fierce opposition, how their older brother and Moran had fought, and when Maggie yielded to Moran and stayed, Luke had gone on his own without telling his father.

She waited until Moran himself had to come to talk about Maggie. Sheila and Mona were at the convent secondary school, Michael was finishing national school. Maggie had so little to do during the day that she spent much of the time chatting and gossiping with Rose. She would pretend to be busy whenever she heard Moran come. 'Daddy hates to see anybody sitting down doing nothing.' 'Poor Daddy,' Rose would smile with affection after he had gone again.

Moran began to see how little Maggie had to do in the house and that she needed money for dances and clothes now. He suspected Rose was letting her have some of her own money.

'Do you still think that Maggie should go to England to nurse?' he asked eventually.

'I do. She'd always have something to fall back on. You never know what is going to happen in a life. It's a profession.'

'I don't know. I was very much against it when that brother of hers wanted her to go. Of course he wasn't interested in what was good or bad for the girls. He was doing it against me.'

'I'm far from against you, you know that. I want it for her own good. This place will always be here for her to come home to as long as I breathe.'

Because of the shortages of girls for nursing, many ads were appearing in the daily papers. Rose helped Maggie to write away for the forms and then to fill in the forms when they came. To Moran's surprise she was accepted for training by five hospitals. The whole house sat down after the Rosary one evening to pick the hospital she would go to. They chose the London Hospital because a few people from around were already working there. After they had reached that decision Michael began to cry and would not be consoled.

'They'll all be gone soon,' he said to their humorous questioning. 'It's awful. It's not fair.'

When Rose suggested that they write to Luke to ask him to meet Maggie off the train when she got to London Moran was furious.

'Didn't the hospital say they'd have her met?'

'He's her brother. It'd be natural for him to meet Maggie.'

'There's not a natural bone in that gentleman's body. I wrote him several times and all the answer I ever got was I'm-well-here-and-I-hope-you-are-well-there. Is that natural after all the years of bringing him up?'

'These things happen in families and then they pass,' Rose said quietly. 'An accident happens or a wedding. People are forced back together again. I know how you feel, Daddy, but maybe it is better not to take too strong a stand. Things are always changing. You never know how they'll turn out. If you do the generous thing, then you can't be blamed.'

'I can be blamed. Make no mistake about that. In this case I can always be blamed.'

'I know it is hard but it's better to try to ignore what is said against you. If you can ignore it then you'll know that you have nothing to blame yourself for. Do nothing in a hurry.'

'What do you want me to do?'

'I think it'd be better if *you* wrote him,' Rose suggested.

'I'll probably just earn another kick in the teeth but I'll do it none the less.'

Moran spent a long time composing the letter. He could not resist adding recrimination. Luke answered the letter by telegram. Seldom a telegram came and nobody liked to see one come to a house. The small green envelope with the harp generally came with news of sudden death. Moran's high-strung nervousness, which was usually concealed by slow, deliberate movements, was all on show as he looked about him like an animal in unknown territory and tore open the envelope. When he read DELIGHTED TO MEET MAGGIE STOP LOVE STOP LUKE he had to struggle to contain himself. He was barely able to conceal his fury until after he paid the postman whom he walked all the way out to the iron gate.

'Maybe he just sent the telegram and a letter will come after a few days,' Maggie tried to soothe.

'No letter will come. It leaves me like a right fool out in the bloody open.'

'I don't know how you can say that, Daddy. You did everything decent,' Rose said.

'Why in the name of the Saviour do you have to put your ignorance on full display,' he turned on her. 'You don't know the first thing about the business, woman.'

That the telegram was formally polite and completely ignored his own attack infuriated Moran. After he had read it aloud he crumpled the note up in his fist and thrust it into the fire as if the very sight of it was hateful.

'Well, at least you'll have someone to meet you at Euston,' Rose said softly to Maggie who already knew that she would be met.

'Of course he'll meet her. He'll meet her to try to turn her against me,' shouted Moran.

'He was polite enough,' Rose suggested.

'What do you know about it? What in hell do you know about anything?'

He swept his hat from the dresser and crushed it on his head and went outside as if he might break down the doors in his way. Soon they heard the sharp, swift sounds of the axe as he started to split lengths of branches into firewood.

She stood stunned. He had never spoken to her like that before. In the spreading lull she looked towards the others. They had all been there when Moran read out the telegram. Part of her expected to find them laughing at his wild reaction beyond all sense and to return her to the blessed normal but when she looked around only Maggie stood in the room. The others had slipped away like ghosts. Maggie was kneading currants through dough in a glass bowl on the sideboard, absorbed in the kneading as if all of her life were passing through the pale dough.

'Where have they all disappeared to all of a sudden, Maggie?'

'They must have gone out,' Maggie looked up from the dough with intense attention.

'I thought I might find them laughing at poor Daddy,' Rose said, allowing her own shock and fear to ease out in the nervous laughter, but Maggie's face remained pale and serious.

'I don't know what happened to Daddy,' Rose said.

'Sometimes he gets like that.'

'I never saw him so upset.'

'He's not been like that for a long time.'

'Was he often like that?'

'Before, but not for a long time now,' Maggie admitted reluctantly and Rose did not want to learn any more. She had already more than she wanted to deal with. In the silence the sound of the sledge could be heard thudding on stones from one of the near fields. He had already abandoned the timber.

Often when talking with the girls she had noticed that whenever Moran entered the room silence and deadness would fall on them; and if he was eating alone or working in the room – setting the teeth of a saw, putting a handle in a broken spade on a wet day, taking apart the lighting plant that never seemed to run properly for long – they always tried to slip away. If they had to stay they moved about the place like shadows. Only when they dropped or rattled something, the startled way they would look towards Moran, did the nervous tension of what it took to glide about so silently show. Rose had noticed this and she had put it down to the awe and respect in which the man she so loved was held, and she was loath to see differently now. She had chosen Moran, had married him against convention and her family. All her vanity was in question. The violence Moran had turned on her she chose to ignore, to let her own resentment drop and to join the girls as they stole about so that their presences would never challenge his.

He came in very late, wary, watchful. The cheerfulness with which Rose greeted him he met with a deep reserve. She was unprepared for it and her nervousness increased tenfold as she bustled about to get his tea. Sheila and Mona were writing at side tables; Michael was kneeling at the big armchair, a book between his elbows, as if in prayer, a position he sometimes used for studying. All three looked up gravely to acknowledge their father's presence; but, sensing his mood at once, they buried themselves again in their schoolwork.

'Where's Maggie?' he demanded.

53

'She went to visit some friends in the village.'

'She seems always to be on the tramp these days.'

'She's going around mostly saying goodbye to people.'

'I'm sure she'll be missed,' he said acidly.

Rose poured him his tea. The table was covered with a spotless cloth. As he ate and drank she found herself chattering away to him out of nervousness, a stream of things that went through her head, the small happenings of a day. She talked out of confusions: fear, insecurity, love. Her instinct told her she should not be talking but she could not stop. He made several brusque, impatient movements at the table but still she could not stop. Then he turned round the chair in a fit of hatred. The children were listening though they kept their eyes intently fixed on their school books.

'Did you ever listen carefully to yourself, Rose?' he said. 'If you listened a bit more carefully to yourself I think you might talk a lot less.'

She looked like someone who had been struck without warning but she did not try to run or cry out. She stood still for a long moment that seemed to the others to grow into an age. Then, abjectly, as if engaged in reflection that gave back only its own dullness, she completed the tasks she had been doing and, without saying a word to the expectant children, left the room.

'Where are you going, Rose?' he asked in a tone that told her that he knew he had gone too far but she continued on her way.

It galled him to have to sit impotently in silence; worse still, that it had been witnessed. They kept their heads down in their books though they had long ceased to study, unwilling to catch his eye or even to breathe loudly. All they had ever been able to do in the face of violence was to bend to it.

Moran sat for a long time. When he could stand the silence no longer he went briskly into the other room. 'I'm sorry, Rose,' they heard him say. They were able to hear clearly though he had closed the door. 'I'm sorry, Rose,' he had to say again. 'I lost my temper.' After a pause they thought would never end they heard, 'I want to be alone,' clear as a single bell note, free of all self-assertiveness. He stayed on in the room but there was nothing he could do but withdraw.

When he came back he sat beside the litter of his meal on the table among the three children not quite knowing what to do with himself. Then he took a pencil and paper and started to tot up all the monies he presently held against the expenses he had. He spent a long time over these calculations and they appeared to soothe him.

'We might as well say the Rosary now,' he announced when he put pencil and paper away, taking out his beads and letting them dangle loudly. They put away their exercises and took out their beads.

'Leave the doors open in case Rose wants to hear,' he said to the boy. Michael opened both doors to the room. He paused at the bedroom door but the vague shape amid the bedclothes did not speak or stir.

At the Second Glorious Mystery Moran paused. Sometimes if there was an illness in the house the sick person would join in the prayers through the open doors but when the silence was not broken he nodded to Mona and she took up Rose's Decade. After the Rosary, Mona and Sheila made tea and they all slipped away early.

Moran sat on alone in the room. He was so engrossed in himself that he was startled by the sound of the back door opening just after midnight. Maggie was even more startled to find him alone when she came in and instantly relieved that she hadn't allowed the boy who had seen her home from the village further than the road gate.

'You're very late,' he said.

'The concert wasn't over till after eleven.'

'Did you say your prayers on the way home?'

'No, Daddy. I'll say them as soon as I go upstairs.'

'Be careful not to wake the crowd that has to go to school in the morning.'

'I'll be careful. Good night, Daddy.' As on every night, she went up to him and kissed him on the lips.

55

He sat on alone until all unease was lost in a luxury of self-absorption. The fire had died. He felt stiff when he got up from the chair and turned out the light and groped his way through the still open doorway to the bed, shedding his clothes on to the floor. When he got into bed he turned his back energetically to Rose.

She rose even earlier than usual next morning. Usually she enjoyed the tasks of morning but this morning she was grateful above all mornings for the constancy of the small demanding chores: to shake out the fire, scatter the ashes on the grass outside, to feel the stoked fire warm the room. She set the table and began breakfast. When the three appeared for school they were wary of her at first but she was able to summon sufficient energy to disguise her lack of it and they were completely at ease before they left for school. When Moran eventually appeared he did not speak but fussed excessively as he put on socks and boots. She did not help him.

'I suppose I should be sorry,' he said at length.

'It was very hard what you said.'

'I was upset over that telegram my beloved son sent. It was as if I didn't even exist.'

'I know, but what you said was still hard.'

'Well then, I'm sorry.'

It was all she demanded and immediately she brightened. 'It's all right, Michael. I know it's not easy.' She looked at him with love. Though they were alone they did not embrace or kiss. That belonged to darkness and the night.

'Do you know what I think, Rose? We get too cooped up here sometimes. Why don't we just go away for the day?'

'Where would we go to?'

'We can drive anywhere we want to drive to. That's the great thing about having a car. All we have to do is back it out of the shed and *go*.'

'Do you think you can spare the day?' She was still careful.

'It's bad if we can't take one day off,' he said laughingly. He was happy now, relieved, pleased with himself, ready to be indulgent.

He backed the Ford out of the shed and faced it to the road. Maggie had risen and was taking breakfast when he came in.

'Is there anything you want, Daddy?'

'Not a thing in the wide world, thanks be to God.' She was relieved to hear the tone. 'You'll have the whole place to yourself today. Rose and myself are away for the day.'

'When do you think you'll be back, Daddy?'

Rose had left out his brown suit and shirt and tie and socks and he had started to dress.

'We'll be back when you see us. We'll be back before night anyhow,' he said as he tucked his shirt into his trousers, hoisting them round his hips.

'I'm holding everybody up,' Rose fussed self-effacingly. She looked well, even stylish in a discreet way, in her tweed suit and white blouse.

'Daddy looks wonderful. I hope I'm not too much of a disgrace,' she laughed nervously, moving her hands and features in one clear plea to please.

'You look lovely, Rose. You look like a lady,' Maggie said.

'I'm bound to be taken for the chauffeur,' he laughed out, mispronouncing the word with relish but he was not corrected as he hoped.

'There'd never be a fear of that,' she said with feeling.

They set off together in the small car, Rose's girlish smiles and waves only accentuating the picture of the happy couple going on a whole day's outing alone together. Maggie watched the car turn carefully out into the main road and then she went and closed the gate under the big yew tree.

Moran drove purposefully. The car crossed the shallow racing river in Boyle, passed the grey walls of the roofless monastery, and it kept on the main road leading across the Curlews. Rose hadn't asked him where they were driving to; she didn't care anyhow: it was enough to be with him in the day.

'O'Neill and O'Donnell crossed here with cannon and horses on the way to Kinsale in one night,' he told her as the car was climbing into the low mountains. 'They were able to cross because the black frost made the ground hard as rock that night.'

He seemed to relax more after he had spoken, to be less fixedly focused on the empty road.

'I suppose some of your own nights when you were on the run were not unlike that,' she ventured into what they had never spoken of.

'No. They were different,' he said not unkindly but it was clear he didn't want to talk about those nights.

'Would you like to go to Strandhill? When the children were young we went there every year.'

'I'd love to see the ocean,' she said. She didn't care where she went or what she saw as long as he was pleased and she was with him. Now most of her pleasure and all of her pain flowed through him. For her there was always a strange excitement in his presence of something about to happen. Nothing was ever still. She felt inordinately grateful when he behaved normally.

'That's the calm sea,' he pointed out the inlet that ran to Ballysadare as they came along the narrow twisting road into Strandhill. 'We all used to swim there. It's more private and safe. The rough sea at the front is dangerous. There was hardly a summer that three or four weren't drownded.'

'It was very good of you to take them to the sea. Hardly anybody else about except the schoolteachers ever thought of taking their children to the sea.'

'I always tried to do the best or what I thought was best. It is not easy to know sometimes. When you think you're right that is the very time it'll fly back in your teeth. Luke wouldn't come to the sea in the finish.'

'All boys growing up get that way,' she said.

'We had to stop selling the turf then,' he said.

'What turf?' she asked.

'We took a lorry load of turf for our own fire and sold the rest in bags door to door.' He pointed out the pebbled street in front of Park's Guest House where they had first stayed and a bungalow they had taken between the church and the golf links. 'We sold the turf from there. It paid for the entire holiday. There was a great take on it. That whole summer was wet. Everybody wanted a fire because of the rain. We made money on that holiday.'

There were only two other cars at the front and they rolled to a stop alongside the plinth on which the antique cannon stood pointing out to sea like some deep-chested mongrel. They sat for a long time in silence watching the Atlantic crash down on the empty shore.

'We haven't come to the sea in three years. I suppose that's how you get old. You find yourself not doing a whole lot of things you once did without a thought.'

'You're not old,' Rose said.

'The mileage is up,' he said. 'You can't turn it back.'

'I wasn't sure what you'd want to do,' Rose said with the utmost caution, 'and I brought a flask of tea and sandwiches just in case.'

'That's great.' He had been dreading having to look for a place for lunch. He knew no cheap place here any more and he would have to search one out like a blind man. 'We can go anywhere we want to afterwards,' he added in case he was appearing stingy.

Rose opened the flask, spreading the sandwiches on the dashboard. 'Bless us, O Lord, and these Thy gifts . . .' He ate and drank with relish, pointing out a fishing boat leaving Sligo harbour, remarking how Rosses Point across the bay had safe bathing while here you couldn't stand in the water without feeling the currents pushing the sand out from under your feet. 'But it's dull at the old Point, Rose. The waves there are small even in a storm. Here you get the real feel of the ocean. That's what I always used to say to the troops.'

'It's a wonderful place,' she said.

'I feel like a new man,' he said as she put the flask away and combed the crumbs from the dashboard into her cupped hand. They both took up together, 'We give Thee thanks, O Almighty God, for all Thy bounty which we have received through Christ Our Lord who liveth and reigneth world without end, amen.'

Cheerfully they got out of the car into the open day and went down the rocks to the strand and then out to the tideline. They walked along the tide's edge for a mile. Rose picked some sea shells and rounded stones and Moran put bits of dilsk in his pocket. They turned back before reaching the roofless church in the middle of the old graveyard out on the edge of land.

'The locals still bury there,' he told her.

They came back along the path that threaded a way between the sand dunes. Some bees were already crawling on the early clover.

'This place will have a lot of tents and caravans and people in a month's time.'

'It's nicer walking here than on the strand. There's a lovely spring in the turf.'

'Except you have to watch for the rabbit holes. You could twist an ankle like nobody's business.'

'Aren't we lucky to have met and to have this whole day to ourselves and the sea and the sky,' Rose said enthusiastically.

'It's our life,' he said harshly. She looked at him carefully. He was changing less predictably than the tide. Soon he would need to vent the anger she felt already gathering, and she was the nearest person. Her life was bound up completely with this man she so loved and whose darkness she feared. They should go home before the whole day was about them in ruins.

'Maybe we should go to one of the hotels for tea or ice-cream?' he asked fretfully, as if somehow sensing her withdrawal.

As if to point out that they were not entirely alone, a man with a white terrier came towards them from behind the sand-hills. He carried a pale bone which he kept throwing out into the dune for the terrier to retrieve. Without speaking he lifted his cap as they passed.

'No,' she said firmly. 'I think we should go home. It's easy to spoil the day by trying to do too much.'

'Are you sure, Rose?'

'I'm certain.'

'We must do this more often, Rose,' he said as he backed the

Ford out from the ornamental cannon. There were now four people on the long wide stretch of strand. They looked small and black against the width of rushing water and pale sand.

'We can but of course it won't be as easy for us to get away once Maggie is gone,' she said it in a pleasant way that sometimes humoured him and sometimes could put his teeth on edge. This time it seemed to please him. He would not have liked it if she seemed to be saying that they could get away any time they wanted to. Anything easy and pleasant aroused deep suspicion and people enjoying themselves were usually less inclined to pay attention to others.

Before the marriage Maggie had been little more than a drudge round the house. Rose set her free. She saw that she had pretty clothes like other girls her age and a little money of her own for going out. She listened to the stories of small triumphs brought back from the dances. Maggie had never received so much attention. With this new confidence she went willingly out to Moran in the fields. She helped him with chores, gathering branches or rounding up cattle, or just stayed to keep him company while he worked.

Soon she was leaving and it was easy for him to be charming. He never scolded except in passing fits of irritation. His instinct was to draw her closer to him. 'Life is a peculiar venture,' he was fond of saying. 'You never know how low or high you'll go. No matter how you rise in the world never look down on another. That way you can never go far wrong.'

'Daddy is great,' Maggie said with pride when she came in.

Rose remained silent but the pleasure showed in her features.

'When he's nice he can be that way,' Mona looked up gravely from her schoolwork.

'It'd be even nicer if he was always that way,' Sheila added tartly.

'Maybe we are not always that good ourselves if we look closer,' Rose countered quickly.

Michael looked up from where he knelt on the floor in front

61

of the old armchair, his books spread out on the chair. When he discovered their attention was not on him he went back to his books.

On Maggie's last night in the house Rose gave a little party. The night before she had stayed out late saying goodbye to all her friends. Her last night belonged to the house.

Moran said the Rosary early, at the end of which he added a prayer for the girl's safekeeping in the world she was about to enter. He said it with a heavy emphasis which brought them all close to tears but the mood was soon scattered by all the joyful preparations Rose had planned.

Bowls of the clear chicken soup they loved were put on the table. A roast chicken followed, with pale stuffing, a hot gravy and masses of floury roast potatoes. Lemonade was poured into glasses and the meal was toasted. 'This is America at home,' Moran boasted. Bowls of trifle followed. 'We'll burst!' He and everybody were happy. Rose wanted to leave the washing-up for morning but the girls insisted on getting it over with. Then they played cards until stifled yawns and missed tricks told them that tiredness was now king. The three who had to go to school in the morning went to bed. After a decent interval Maggie followed them.

'You'll have a long day tomorrow,' Rose encouraged.

'God bless you and keep you safe,' Moran said.

Maggie looked at him with the light of love as she kissed him good night. He was her first man, her father, as she faced for London and the further opening of her life.

The next day on the platform of the little station he was very fine. He dressed carefully in the brown suit he had been married in and he bought the ticket with quiet authority. As he wasn't friendly with anyone present he had no occasion to speak to others waiting about on the white gravel. Rose knew many of the people on the platform even though she had spent half her life in Scotland and she responded to each greeting with warmth, careful to watch that her friendliness did not grate on Moran. Maggie was silent. She too, in spite of the dances and concerts they had been attending lately, knew far fewer people at the station than Rose. Maggie looked on this isolation he had built up around them as distinction and strength. In her heart she felt that Rose was a little common in knowing so many people. Moran stood erect and apart on the platform, totally separate as he gazed at the hill across the tracks where the stationmaster's brown horse and a few cattle and sheep grazed.

Rose kept touching Maggie as they waited, sometimes kneading her shoulder and arm. 'Look at the fine girl we have. You need have no fear facing the world,' as if she were already clearly seeing her happiness and her children in the fullness of the years.

As the diesel train came in and people were already picking up suitcases from the platform Moran turned and kissed her as if it were a last good night to all the nights she had come to him.

'Remember, the house you left will always be your house. While Rose and I are here you'll have one home that you can always come back to.'

'We'll be looking out for you,' Rose said as they kissed.

Maggie wept. As the train pulled out of the station she searched back for Moran's face among the crowd and found it and waved.

'Do you think that gentleman will meet her?'

'Of course he'll meet her. He's not going to let her wander round London on her own. He's her brother.'

'I wish I could be as certain but I asked the hospital to meet her as well just in case. If for no other reason, he'll probably meet her just to get back at me.'

Even on very wet days Moran seldom hung about the house. He had converted one of the outhouses into a sort of workshop where he tinkered with a collection of small engines, antique lighting plants and water pumps that he had bought for next to nothing at country auctions over the years. He had neither the patience nor method to understand properly how they worked and he would not bow to any instruction other than his own perusal of certain manuals and textbooks. Quite often though, through various hit-and-miss applications, he would get one of the engines running. Then he would be very happy, his natural energy spreading that happiness out to everything around him. Rose shared those sort of days with him even more extravagantly than if the days had been her own. There were many other days when nothing would work for him and every space on the long blackened workbench would be covered with a confusion of parts. Those days Rose dreaded and fretted through and it was a kind of peace to turn to the two girls and the boy. She had won them over completely. They would chat away to her about their day until they got down to the schoolwork. Both girls were exceptionally good at school and fond of study. In their earlier years schoolwork had been a haven. They felt safe and protected when they studied.

Michael too was good at school but only did the minimum of study. After less than a half-hour of sitting alone he would grow restless, scatter his books untidily about the table and disappear outside. 'Are you finished so soon?' Rose would call teasingly but he would have gone with a slam of the door. 'If he's finished you'd think he'd have the manners not to leave the table in such a mess,' the girls would grumble; but they or Rose would always put his books away. Though tall and strong for his age he had no liking for hard physical work and he was slow to give Moran any help on the land. He had several pets: a grey cat Maria, Shep the sheepdog who went everywhere with him over the fields, several birds including a lame pigeon that he loved to tease Maria with; and one spring he reared a wild duck from the egg of an abandoned nest and was upset for weeks after the October day it finally flew away. Rose started a small flower garden in front of the house soon after coming and there he could often be found, at first helping Rose, then taking over and extending the garden across the footpath until all the green inside the thorn hedge was alive with colour: little beds of forget-me-nots and sweet william, rows of wallflowers that gave out their fragrance in the evenings, formal lilies and roses. His way with birds and animals seemed to go out to all flowers and plants, too. This both amused and irritated Moran.

'I suppose one of these days you'll be getting yourself a skirt.'

'Trousers are far handier,' he was able to smile it aside.

'If you grew something like carrots it'd make some sense. It'll be a long time before you'd eat any of those flowers.'

'They're fun to look at.'

'Looking won't get you far in this world,' Moran said.

But hidden in the boy's answering nod was an equal contempt for Moran's work, which he regarded as nothing short of voluntary slavery. Brought up from infancy by a screen of girls, and now growing confidently in Rose's shade, he escaped the fear of Moran.

After Maggie went away Moran took up his old habit of going to the post office. As he no longer wrote to relatives or old war comrades, he explained stiffly, 'I'm expecting word from my daughter in London. Young people abroad can be quite heedless nowadays.' Evening after evening passed by without Annie the postmistress finding a letter for him in the grey bag the mail van brought in. Eventually when the letter came in its blue envelope with the pious *SAG* printed across the seal, the hands so firm holding a gun or tool shook as he took it. Annie was annoyed by the abrupt way he turned away and went out. Outside on the footpath he stood like a stone reading the letter. People leaving the post office spoke to him but he did not hear. When at last he moved away he still combed through the letter as he walked. By the time he got to the house he knew each phrase by heart.

'She stirred herself at last and wrote,' he said as he handed Rose the letter.

'She'd have a lot to get used to at first,' Rose said absently as she scanned through the letter. Luke had met her at Euston. They had gone to the hospital by the Underground. All the student nurses each had a small room with a desk and bed in the nurses' home. There were several Irish girls in the class and two girls from near Ballymote. She was just beginning to get used to the wards and the classes. There was a big park with

65

a lake not far from the hospital. Last Sunday Luke had come out. They had gone to the park. Boats were for hire by the hour and they had rowed on the lake. Afterwards they had tea in a wooden café beside the lake. She sent lots of love and a whole line of kisses.

'You'd think after all that that she'd say what his lordship was actually doing in London.'

'Still, he met her and went to see her on Sunday.'

'He'd do that. Yes. He'd do that all right.'

'Maybe she didn't get round to asking him much about himself yet,' Rose said just to break the brooding silence.

'Maggie may be slow but she's not that slow,' he said impatiently. 'Your man warned her not to say anything about what he is doing. That's why she wrote nothing.'

Carelessly he let a page of newspaper fall on the cement beside the table and spilled his beads from the small purse into his palm. He prayed absentmindedly, never able to fall into the even, sleepy drone and hum of 'Our Father' and 'Hail Mary'. He even made a number of slips and repetitions that on a different evening he would have been quick to reprimand in others. Before he had put his beads away he was in search of pen and paper and spent till late writing to Maggie. He had a clean, bare style; when writing he seemed to be able to slip the burden of his personality as he could never do face to face. The three children had gone to bed and Rose was waiting by the fire by the time he was satisfied enough with what he had written to seal the envelope.

With Maggie in London, Sheila and Mona had more light to themselves and were better able to come into their own. Sheila was more than good at school, impulsive and assertive, yet she withdrew into a shell at a hint of opposition. After school Rose loved to draw her out, to tease out of her reckless opinions and to watch her quick mind wheel and tack as she strained to defend what was usually insupportable. Mona was quiet, hardworking and extremely stubborn, anxious to be agreeable; but once she took up a position – or got caught in one – she was obstinately immovable and this had often brought her into conflict with Moran. Rose's coming to the house had smoothed their lives and allowed them to concentrate everything on school and study, which, above all, they saw as a way out of the house and into a life of their own.

Eventually a letter arrived from London in response to Moran's exasperated inquiries about his elder son. The information could hardly have been more ordinary. Maggie had seen him nearly every day at first. Now she saw him much less. When he first came, he had worked on various building sites. Now he worked in offices of the Gas Board, and was studying accountancy, mostly at night, though the Board gave him one day off each week to attend classes. Also he had become friendly with a Cockney man, older than he, who had been a french polisher and who now sold reproduction furniture to antique shops from a van. He mentioned some plan they had of buying old houses and converting them into flats for sale.

'You see, it didn't take him long to find the riff-raff,' Moran said.

'He seems to be working hard enough and studying,' Rose tried to reassure him as always from a careful distance.

'He'd do that all right but look at what he's getting mixed up with as well.'

'It may be just talk,' she ventured edgily.

'How does anything start but in talk?'

Outwardly it had been the easiest and quietest of times that the house had ever known but the unease did not go away. Increasingly Moran could be seen in the fields staring idly at some task he should be completing.

The fierce rush of hay was over. The apples were ripening on the trees in the garden. Their eyes were turning towards winter. Rose was beginning to go regularly again to her mother's house. The cane basket on the handlebars of her bicycle was always full on leaving the house and full again with things from her mother's house when she came back.

'I see there's hardly a day nowadays that Rose doesn't go to her relations,' Moran said to Sheila and Mona one Saturday they brought him a flask of tea into the fields. 'She seldom goes

67

empty-handed.' Rose had asked them to take the flask out to him at four. They knew she took bread to her mother, jam she had made from the blackcurrants at the foot of the garden but the basket always came back heavy with fresh eggs, a bunch of carrots from the bog, plums that they loved, sweet hard yellow apples.

'We don't know,' Sheila answered carefully.

'How do you not know? Haven't you both eyes in your heads?'

'She brings things back.'

'Only stuff they'd have to throw out otherwise!'

They knew that the accusation was untrue. They remained obstinately silent, abject looking as well, the camouflage they had learned to use for safekeeping.

'Would you like us to tie the sheaves, Daddy?' Mona asked.

'That'd be a great push,' he said.

All the girls were skilled at farm work, work they had done since they were very young. Quickly the rows were gathered into sheaves and tied. They loved the sound of swishing the sheaves made as they were stooked, the clash of the tresses of hard grain against grain, the sight of the rich ears of corn leaning delicately out on the shoulders of the stooks.

'That was great,' Moran said. 'What's left is only trimming. I can do that myself. I am sure ye have books,' he added with unusual thoughtfulness.

'Thanks, Daddy.'

'Thanks yourselves.' And then he added, 'We could get on topping without her.'

It was not so much that she took things from the house – though his racial fear of the poorhouse or famine was deep – but that she left the house at all. Any constant going out to another house was a threat. In small things it showed. The shaving water was boiling. Did she want to scald the face off a man? God, O God, O God, did she not know anything? Look at the holes in these socks. 'Where, O God, is that woman now? Has a whole army to be sent out to search for you whenever you're needed?'

She did not try to defend herself. 'Coming, Daddy. Coming,' she would call, often arriving breathless. Not once did she protest at the unfairness. She seemed willing to go to almost any length to appease, lull his irritation to rest, contain all the exasperation by taking it within herself. This usually redoubled it. He seemed intent now on pushing to see how far he could go and she appeared willing to give way in everything in order to pacify.

The children were deeply ashamed: 'He used to be like that when Luke was here, Rose; only it was worse.'

'These flare-ups happen in every family. It is easy to exaggerate. I'm sure Daddy never meant any harm. These things can be taken too much to heart.' She would not hear the accusation.

'It's true what Mona says.'

'Now, these things can be exaggerated out of all proportion. Daddy may act like that – none of us are all that good – but he never means it. I know how much he loves everybody in the house.'

'It's just not fair.'

'You should know you'll not change your father now and he means everything for the best for the whole house,' she argued forcibly but the strain was showing on her own drawn, anxious features.

Then one evening as she was tidying up the room he said as quietly as if he were taking rifle aim, 'There's no need for you to go turning the whole place upside down. We managed well enough before you ever came round the place.'

She did not try to answer or to turn it aside. It was again as if she had been struck, her hands barely moving along the surface of the dresser she had been wiping clean of dust, her head going low, and when she finished she went to put the damp cloth carefully beside the sink, moving a simmering saucepan from the hotplate. Such was the slowness and enclosedness of all her movements that the girls instinctively looked up from their school books to follow her closely. Moran watched every move under cover of reading the newspaper. Then, with the same shocking slowness, without a word, without looking at anyone, she went to the door, opened it, and let it close softly behind her. They heard her open and close the bedroom door likewise. There was complete silence.

Moran rattled the newspaper a few times but by the time he could look around the three children were locked back into their school books. After a while Moran tired of looking at the newspapers and went outside though it was almost night.

'What happened?' Michael asked laughingly, hoping to make light of what had taken place.

'Rose went to bed,' Mona answered without looking up from her books and though the boy thought about it for a while he did not ask anything further.

When Moran came back he was even more restless. He went through the newspaper again. Then he got pen and writing pad and sat at the table. He deliberated for a long time in front of the pad, and then suddenly rose and put it away without writing anything.

'We better say the prayers,' he said, taking his beads from the leather purse. As they prepared to kneel he added, 'Open the doors in case Rose wants to hear.' Mona went and opened both doors. At the bedroom door she called softly, 'Rose, we're starting the Rosary.' But not even a whisper came from the room. Mona came in. 'The doors are open,' and took her place without looking at anyone.

'Thou, O Lord, wilt open my lips.'

'And my tongue shall announce Thy praise,' their response was like a muted echo.

The doors stayed open but no murmur came from the other room. Moran paused after the First Decade. Rose always recited the Second Decade but when no sound whatever came from the room he nodded severely to Mona to begin. On the completion of the circle, Moran again had to recite the Last Decade. 'Will we shut the doors, Daddy?' Mona asked nervously after they rose from their knees.

'What does it matter whether they are open or shut?' he said and the doors remained open.

As soon as they finished with their books the two girls made him tea. Rose always made tea at this hour. Immediately after they tidied and washed up, they went to kiss Moran good night and slipped away to their rooms. He sat for more than an hour alone before dragging himself to the room, shutting the doors loudly behind him as he went. He did not speak in the room, allowing his clothes to fall on to the floor in the darkness, waiting for some stir or sign from Rose, but the only sound in the room was the brushing of his own clothes falling in the darkness.

'Are you awake at all there, Rose?' he whispered before reaching out to pull aside the bedclothes.

She did not answer at first but moved or turned.

'I'm awake,' she said at last in a voice strained with hurt. 'I'll have to go away from here.'

'I never heard such nonsense,' he blustered. 'Are you taking everything up as serious as some of the other people in the house? Does every move have to be Judgement Day?'

'I was told I was no use in the house. I couldn't go on living in a place where I was no use,' she spoke with the quietness and desperate authority of someone who had discovered they could give up no more ground and live.

'God, O God. Has everything to be taken like this? I never meant anything like that. The whole world knows that the house was never run right until you came. A blind man could see that the children think the earth of you. They'd cry their eyes out if they heard even a whisper of this silly talk.'

'It didn't sound silly to me. It sounded as if it was meant. I'll have to go back to Glasgow and take up my life there again.'

'God, can't a man say anything in his own house without it being taken up wrong?' and the quarrel circled about the two positions until he reached and took her in his arms. She neither yielded to him nor attempted to pull away.

'I love you dearly and I love the house but I couldn't live here if I am not wanted.'

'I thought we'd finished with that for ever.' He was restless by her side, clenching and unclenching his hands. He had been checked. Instead of recognition, all that the quarrel had incurred

71

was a deepening blindness. He now knew less about her than the day they had first met in the post office, standing beside one another on the scrubbed hollow boards, waiting for the evening mail van to come.

Mona and Sheila rose earlier than usual the next morning. They had heard noises of someone rising very early and felt apprehensive. They weren't sure if they would find Rose there at all or what way they would find her if they did. They were taken aback to find her smiling and totally at ease. The room was already warm and the furniture shone as if all the pieces had been gone over with a damp cloth.

'You are all up a bit before your time. You could have stolen another few minutes,' she said as if the evening had never happened. She poured their tea and sat with a cup of her own by the fire, chatting away as easily as she did every morning. 'No danger of your brother ever getting up too early,' she said and went to call Michael. When he came into the room, sleepy and rubbing his eyes, he too stared as if not able to believe how like all other mornings the morning was. Nothing seemed to have changed.

Moran stayed in bed until late that day, disappearing silently into the fields after eating. When the children came back from school they found that still nothing had changed. Moran was in a rage about tools and a barrow that had been left out in the rain and complained about how much money was being wasted heedlessly about the house all the time.

'Why does he always have to go on like that?' Sheila was emboldened from what she saw the night before to ask Rose when Moran had gone out again.

'Daddy worries. He worries a great deal about the house.' Rose said it with such empathy that all criticism was stopped. All they could do was to look at her but no one could read Rose's face and they turned back to their books. They were only weeks away from the examinations halls. So much work still had to be done, so much work had to be gone over again. The chance-throw of the exam would almost certainly determine the quality of much of the rest of their lives. Sheila especially had dreams of university. Much could be won, a great deal more could be lost, and there was always England.

At this time Moran ordered an enormous load of lime that blocked the avenue. To cut down on expense he did not get the big factory spreaders but started to spread it himself with tractor and shovel. For days he backed the little transport box into the huge mound and went up and down the fields in lines, stopping the tractor every few yards to scatter the lime, tossing each shovelful on the wind for the white dust to be blown out over the grass. No matter how carefully he sliced each shovelful in an arc out on the wind, there were certain unpredictable gusts that lifted the grains and blew them back towards the tractor so that by evening his clothes were filthy with lime, his face and hands as white as chalk, accentuating the inflamed red round his eyes. The theatrical paleness of his face and hands pleased him. 'I'm a boody man,' he pretended to chase Rose and the children with his old charm. Rose was delighted, the clowning bringing relief back into the house after the hidden battle. It would never be over but Rose's place in the house could never be attacked or threatened again. 'I'm a boody man. I'm a boody man,' he made playful sallies to left and right while everybody pretended to back away, shouting and laughing.

As the days went by and the busy little transport box seemed to be making only slow way into the huge heap of lime, he no longer eased it out on the blade of the shovel for the wind to take it but scattered it anywhere out of sight, anywhere to be rid of it. More often because of his impatience, it blew back in his face, dusting him all over. Each night he would be more red-eyed, hardly able to drag his feet with tiredness, his face caked white with lime, lime in his eyes and ears and nostrils, his throat dry, lime thick through his hair and clothes and when he sat down to the table he felt as if he were eating lime.

The blindman's buff of 'I'm the boody man' was gone and they served his tiredness with careful silence. Rose bent over him with pure attention.

'Do you think it will rain?' he asked Rose.

'The forecast is for the same dry hard weather for days.'

'If it rains,' he said gloomily, 'if it rains that heap will set like mixed concrete and we'll never be rid of it'; and though there was no sign of a break in the weather he covered the slowly diminishing heap at night with clear plastic, weighted down with stones.

The girls were now too close to their exam, too anxious to do more than lift their faces to him, but out of the tiredness and filth of lime he could be seen looking often at their heads bent over the lamplit pages in what looked close to melancholy and sunken reflection.

'I was in the eighth class in Moyne,' he said and named four boys in the same class. 'It was as far as you could go in Moyne. I was there for two years. All the others went on to be priests. Joe Brady became a Bishop in Colorado. He died two years ago. I used to write to him till then. You couldn't go further than the eighth class without going on to be a priest.'

'Even if you had money?' Rose asked.

'No one had money round Moyne,' he smiled, aching with tiredness, filthy and white with lime. 'We were all good in the eighth class in Moyne but I was the best in maths.' He named the others who shone in different subjects. 'They all went on to be priests and then the Troubles started and I left too. Strange, to this day I have never met a priest who wasn't afraid to die. I could never make head or tails of that. It flew in the face of everything.'

'If it had been a different time you'd have been a doctor or an engineer,' Rose said.

'I wouldn't have been a doctor,' he shivered with tiredness, ill at ease by the very suggestion of a shape other than his own. 'These lassies will be worn out with all this study,' Moran changed.

'No, Daddy. We're just going over something again for the exam.'

'We've had good weather for weeks now. You're all day inside in school. You should take your books into the fresh air.' He returned to it again and again, the good weather held and they were compelled eventually to go outside. They went to

74

Oakport Woods, leaving their bicycles at the big iron gate, and walking with their books over the grass to the belt of trees along Oakport Lake. The late May sun burned overhead. It would be cool and dark within the wood and there was a cold spring.

'I don't know why he had to rout us out. We have wasted all this time getting here. We'd study better at home,' Sheila complained crossing the fields.

'That's him,' Mona answered. 'He's never content with things the way they are.'

They passed the delicate white blossoms of wild cherry, Sheila striding along in angry resentment, Mona following in her shadow. The light of water showed through the tree trunks as they drew close to the narrow wood along the lake but once on the fringe of the trees they lost all resentment at the sight of the thick floor of bluebells beneath the trees. To advance further into the wood was to trample on the colour blue.

'There must be thousands.'

'There's millions!'

Their feet left clear tracks through the floor of bluebells as if on dark snow, the soft stems crushing to pulp under their feet. At the well they left their books and went down to the shore. The water was still. Summer had not yet replaced the wheaten reeds of winter with green along the edges. Out in the lake the gulls wheeled and scolded above their young on the pile of reeds ringed with rocks that formed Seagull Island. There was no boat any longer in Nutley's boathouse. Some boards had been torn from the side and its black paint of tar had turned pale.

'I don't like this place,' Sheila said.

'Do you remember when we used to go with Daddy in the boat on Saturdays?'

'How could I forget!' Sheila said derisively.

Before getting down to their books they searched out a hollow straw and leaned flat across the spring to drink the water which was famed for its coldness. It was as if by drinking from the cold spring they were hoping to appease some spirit of the place so that it wouldn't turn unfriendly to their studies; but they could not settle as they tried to read and make notes. A fly landed on a nose. A pure white butterfly tossed about in the light on the edge of the lake. Bees were moving about on the bluebells. A wren or robin scrambled about in a clump of thorns and seemed to be scolding.

'This is a joke,' Sheila closed her book. 'I can't take in a word here. I'm going home. What can he say? It's too close to the exam to waste time.'

'He can't say that we didn't make an attempt.' Mona too was glad to leave.

'We should have known better,' came the exasperated response.

Even Sheila grew a little afraid as they drew close to the house. Coming home so early might seem to be confronting Moran.

'You are almost back before you left.' He met them at the gate and was smiling. 'There's nothing like the lake and the open air for powdering through the lessons.'

'We got nothing done, Daddy.' Sheila hung her head despondently low.

'I'm surprised. I thought when I saw the pair of you coming that you had just raced through everything,' Moran laughed. There was no reason to be afraid; on the contrary, he was delighted.

'There were too many things to look at, Daddy,' Mona said apologetically.

'Ye are making excuses now,' he teased. 'You're just no good and weren't able to make yourselves get down to it.'

After they had gone in and resumed their grind in the usual places, Rose came out to him and said gently, 'You were terrible, Daddy, to make them go down to the lake.'

'What's so terrible about it?' he laughed, still in good humour. 'It's fresh air, isn't it? They need to be rooted out of themselves from time to time. All work and no play makes Jack a dull boy. They'll appreciate the inside of the house far better now.'

This small disturbance did not deflect them for long. They read and reread, often looking quite abstracted, memorizing

76

passages silently, their eyes far off; and when ideas eluded or baffled them they would turn to one another for help, each sister seeming to draw strength and comfort from the other's closeness.

Moran felt so outside their circle of concentration that he had to resort to tiptoeing into the room in an exaggerated parody of someone trying to enter unheard but his only audience was the boy, and that not often, and laughter only lifted the girls' heads from their books for a forgotten moment.

Each of these clear days of scattered apple and white pear tree blossom moved inexorably towards the first day when they set out without books and came home in the evening showing the pink or blue papers they had tested themselves against in the examination hall.

'How do you think you did?' Moran was waiting anxiously to ask each evening.

'We don't know, Daddy. The nun thinks we didn't do too bad.'

'Never mind. We'll always have enough to eat here anyhow,' he said, feeling vulnerable in the face of the power that rested in the hands of the outside.

Then, suddenly, the exams were over. They could put their books away. But, instead of the freedom and ease they had longed for, all they felt was emptiness where once all was tension and work. They had to pass idle days of waiting that stretched ahead to an eternity of weeks in August.

'You don't have to worry about anything,' Moran said constantly. 'You don't have to worry about a single thing.'

In early July the waiting was broken by the excitement of Maggie coming home for the first time since she had left for London. She was coming home for three whole weeks and by the time she left for London again the exam results would be nearly due.

Rose had already started to paint the main room of the house during the first exam. The freed girls helped her finish it, scrub tables and chairs. The old furniture was left outside in the sun to air. They scrubbed white the boards of the floor and the old

77

brown flagstones of the hallway took on a damp glow. Michael's front garden was beautiful with stock, beds of sweet william and marigolds that took greedily the sun from the other flowers – pansies, roses and lilies. Moran washed and polished the car, even cleared rusted machinery from around the house. He was more excited than anyone else and continually cracked jokes.

On the arrival day he considered going to meet Maggie in Carrick but he was afraid that he might miss her and decided to go to Boyle. He left alone before the train reached Carrick. Against Rose's chidings he went in his old working clothes as if, perversely, to deny that the day was special in any way. 'She'll have to take me as she finds me. She's back in the country now.' After he left everyone was glued to the clock.

'The train is coming into Carrick!'

The waiting silence was broken by, 'I'd say the train is leaving Carrick now,' and they all went to the fields behind the house to catch a glimpse of the train as it passed. They heard the diesel engine, the quick rattle of the wheels on rails and then the caterpillar of carriages that rose above the stone walls, the small windows flashing in the sun as they were quickly drawn across their view and gone. Then they all moved to the front of the house to watch the road and wait.

They were so intent on watching every car that they failed to pick up Moran's until it was turning slowly in the gate under the yew tree. Moran looked stern and self-conscious as he drove up the short avenue. Maggie burst into tears at the sight of the house and the small familiar crowd waiting for her outside the wooden gate of the garden. Everyone embraced blindly and kissed one by one.

'You are such a handsome one now,' Rose looked her up and down with pleasure.

'What do you think of an old fellow like myself turning up to meet such a grand lassie?'

Rose laughed and there was a general scramble to carry the baggage into the house.

In the house Maggie unpacked the presents she brought: a brilliant red woollen scarf for Rose, a brown V-necked pullover for Moran; Sheila and Mona were handed silken headscarves and Michael a saffron tie to go with his hair. She also brought him seeds with pictures of the flowers on the packets.

'Do you think they will grow here?' he asked, impressed that they had come all the way from London.

A big box of soft-centred chocolates was handed round. Tea was made. She was the centre of the table. They asked her greedily about London.

'What's Luke like now?' Sheila burst out.

Silence fell at once. Everyone looked towards Moran who held his own pained silence.

'He's just the same,' Maggie said and continued on about the nurses' home while Sheila bit her tongue.

Such was the excitement and focus on Maggie that in spite of Rose's care to draw him into the conversation Moran began to feel out of it and grew bored.

'I think it's time to say the Rosary,' he said earlier than usual, taking out his beads. They put newspapers down and knelt. This night Moran enunciated each repetitious word with a slow clarity and force as if the very dwelling on suffering, death and human supplication would scatter all flimsy vanities of a greater world; and the muted responses giving back their acceptance of human servitude did not improve his humour. The coughing, the rustling of the newspapers, the rasp of coat buttons on table or chair exasperated his brooding. The high spirits round the tea table had gone. Then, like a shoal of fish moving within a net, Rose and the girls started to clear the table, to brush away crumbs, to wash, to dry, to return each thing to its own place, all done with a muted energy; whispers, jokes, little scolding asides – 'No, that goes in the other place' or reminisce how they had made the same mistake before in order to soften any harshness in the scold, bending low in apologetic laughter. Ingratiating smiles and words were threaded in and out of the whole whirl of busyness. Amid it all was their constant awareness of Moran's watching presence, sharpening everything they did with the danger of letting something fall and break and bring the weight of his disapproval into the small chain. All their movements were based more on habit and instinct and fear than any real threat but none the less it was an actual physical state. They would wash up the same way even if they were not watched.

As looking down from great heights brings the urge to fall and end the terror of falling, so his very watching put pressure on them to make a slip as they dried and stacked the plates and cups. There were several alarms, bringing laughing giggles of relief when they came to nothing. Then they quietly washed and dried their own hands and returned to the general room. Moran sat on, brooding in the car chair, his thumbs idly revolving around one another.

'I think we should have a cup of tea,' Rose said with jollying encouragement towards Moran but when he only looked back out at her she just continued talking as she got kettle and teapot. 'Maggie will want an early night. I know how tired she must be after the journey. That night boat is the worst of all, and the waiting.' Whether it was the suggestion or pure tiredness Maggie was yawning as if in her support.

The girls rose late the following morning. Moran had gone out already into the fields. During the long luxurious breakfast Maggie told Rose and Sheila and Mona more details of her life in London than she was able to the night before – the parties, the dances, the different bands and singers, the boys she met, her girlfriends.

Rose had her own girlhood in Glasgow to share. Mona and Sheila were so poised on the edge of their own lives that they listened as if hearing about the living stream they were about to enter. After the long breakfast the three girls went out to visit Moran in the fields.

They had worked so hard as children in the fields that each field and tree had become a dear presence, especially the hedges. Maggie looked for the old damson tree by McCabe's, the crab and wild cherry. The sky overhead was cloudless. No wind stirred. Small birds flitted in the shade of the branches and bees were crawling over the red and white clover. They found Moran by the sound of malleting. He was replacing broken stakes in a barbed-wire fence in one of the meadows. The sight of his daughters in sleeveless dresses was relief from the lonely tedium of the work.

'I'm planning to knock this meadow before the evening is out,' he told them before they left and joked, 'You'll have to harden your hands before you leave.'

'They are not that soft, Daddy.'

As they walked away from him through the greenness, the pale blue above them, Maggie said, her voice thick with emotion, 'Daddy is just lovely when he's like that.'

'There's nobody who can hold a candle to him,' Mona added. The girls in their different ways wanted to gather their father and the whole, true, heartbreaking day into their arms.

By evening Moran's mood had completely turned again. He changed his boots and clothes in downcast silence and ate without speaking. Whatever was bothering him was gnawing at him as he ate. They knew him so well that everyone fell into a hush and appeared to move around him on tiptoes.

'Do you ever see that brother of yours at all?' he asked without looking up as he finished, drawing his chair roughly back from the table.

'I do but not all that much.'

'How do you mean not all that much?'

'He met me at the station . . .'

'God, don't you think I know that?'

'He came out to the hospital every weekend after I first came but since then it's only every so often he comes out. Once I met him in the West End and we went to the pictures.' Maggie wanted to please and pacify him on this her holiday at any cost.

'How does he look?'

'He looks fine. He looks no different than when he was here.'

'Did you mention when you wrote that he is in with some Cockney riff-raff?'

'It's something to do with converting old houses. I'm not certain what it is.'

'Believe me, he wouldn't tell what it is.'

'He goes to night school though,' she defended uneasily.

'Doing what?'

'Accountancy. He'll be qualified before too long.'

'Does he ask about us at all?'

'He asks if we have any news.'

'Does he ever talk about coming home?'

'No.'

'And did he not send any word to anybody when he knew you were coming home?'

'Yes. He sent word. He wishes everybody the best.'

'God, I don't know what's wrong with this house,' Moran rose, preparing to go out. 'Getting information from anybody is like trying to extract teeth.'

'We don't know any more than that,' Maggie protested to Rose after he had gone. 'I told Daddy everything we know about Luke.'

'Don't worry,' Rose hushed. 'Daddy's like that. He takes all these things far too seriously.'

When he came in for the night some hours later he was still agitated and fretting. 'I don't know,' he said as he sat to the table. 'I don't know what I did to deserve it. I don't know why things can't be the same in this house as in every other house in the country. I don't know why it is always *me* that has to be singled out.'

Rose fussed discreetly around him but he could not remain the centre of attention for long. Maggie was going to a dance and she was taking Mona and Sheila. All three girls were dressing and their youthful excitement pulsed through the house. Rose too was caught up in the preparations.

'Be careful,' Moran advised when he kissed each of them in turn as they were ready to leave. 'Be careful never to do anything to let yourselves or the house down.'

'We'd never do that, Daddy.'

'Enjoy yourselves,' Rose advised them simply.

After they had gone a complete silence that only reflected itself settled down like lead and was broken only by the sound of Moran removing his boots to go to bed early.

The next morning the girls woke to the incessant clatter of the mowing arm circling the big meadow. Moran had started to mow. All hands would be needed. Whatever leisure the holidays had promised was now ended. The whole house would be consumed by the fever of haytime, the fear of broken weather until every wisp was won.

'The big meadow is down. It'll be all hands on deck from now on,' Moran told the girls as they sat over a late breakfast. He was happy and relieved that the first part of the mowing was completed without any breakage.

'It'll be great if the rain keeps off,' Rose said.

'It might take the edge off the dancing,' Moran teased. 'You'll be too tired to dance tonight anyhow.'

'That might not be a bit of harm!' they smiled back.

As soon as the dew had been burned off the grass, the whole house was in the hayfield, shaking out the heavy tangled lumps of grass the tedder had missed with the fork, raking what was light in from the edges. Towards evening, when the grass started to take on the dry crackle of hay, it was as if the small handshakings were springing up in the meadow. The weather did not look like breaking. Moran put the mowing arm back on the tractor and cut the second and third meadows. They had most of the big meadow up by nightfall. By then every muscle ached, and it was with deep gratitude that they turned at last to drag their feet towards the house. 'There'll surely be no dancing tonight.' 'You can say that twice over.'

They were stiff as boards the next morning. When they moved, every muscle ached but by midday they were in the fields again. Rose and Michael brought tea and sandwiches out to the field. Moran was either mowing a new field or tossing the field ahead of them with the tedder but he joined the band of girls under the shade of one of the big beeches when Rose came with the basket and can.

'It can't be helped, it must be done,' he said after they had eaten and rested. Rose gathered up what was left of the sandwiches of tinned salmon and sardines. The girls rose stiffly in the green shade and turned to the sunlit meadow. Maggie and

Mona were good workers. They worked silently, hardly ever looking up. Sheila hated the work. She complained of blisters on her hands and was forever making forages to the house to escape the backbreaking tedium. The boy worked in fits and bursts, especially in response to praise from Rose. Other times he stood discouraged until shouted at by Moran to do more than just stand there occupying bloody space with everybody killing themselves. Then he would lift his fork angrily and pretend to work. Rose alone was able to laugh and chat away with Maggie and at the same time get through more work than anybody else in the field.

For five whole glaring days they worked away like this, too tired and stiff at night to want to go anywhere but to bed. They had all the hay won except the final meadow when the weather broke. The girls never thought they would lift their faces to the rain in gratitude. They watched it waste the meadows for the whole day.

'To hell with it. We're safe now anyhow. If we don't get the last meadow itself it will do for bedding. Only for the whole lot of you we'd not be near that far on,' Moran was able to praise.

'It was for nothing, Daddy.'

'It was everything. Alone we might be nothing. Together we can do anything.'

Rose put down a big fire against the depression of the constant rain. Everybody in the house loved to move in the warmth and luxury of it, to look out from the bright room at the rain spilling steadily down between the trees. When they moved away from the fire to the outer rooms the steady constant drip of rain from the eaves in the silence was like peace falling.

Now they could dance with a clear conscience. The big regatta dances in the huge grey tent down by the quay in Carrick were just beginning but there were so few days left of the holiday that Maggie preferred to spend them about the house chatting with Rose or her sisters around the fire or talking with Michael out in the front garden among his flowerbeds; and sometimes during long breaks in the rain they would go out to where Moran was tidying up in the meadows.

By the time Maggie had to go back to London they had never felt closer in warmth, even happiness. The closeness was as strong as the pull of their own lives; they lost the pain of individuality within its protection. In London or Dublin the girls would look back to the house for healing. The remembered light on the empty hayfields would grow magical, the green shade of the beeches would give out a delicious coolness as they tasted again the sardines between slices of bread: when they were away the house would become the summer light and shade above their whole lives.

'If we don't do well in the exam, if we don't get anything here,' Sheila blurted out, as they said goodbye outside the front garden while Moran waited with the engine running to drive Maggie to the station, 'you may see us in London soon enough.'

Such was their anxiety during the two days that were left before the exam results were due that Mona and Sheila found it hard to eat or sleep.

'Waiting is the worst,' Rose said sympathetically as she saw them struggling with food. 'Once you see what's in the envelopes everything will be all right.'

'I don't know. I don't know,' Sheila said impatiently.

'They might be dreadful.'

'No they won't. Nothing is so bad as having to imagine.'

So as not to have to watch the empty road for the postman on the day that the results were due each girl went separately deep into the fields but they weren't able to stay alone for long; and each time they came back to the road it was still empty. When at last they did see him coming they had to follow his slow path from the road, watch him lean his bicycle carefully against the wall under the yew and plod slowly up between the two rows of boxwood. Moran who had been watching as anxiously as the two girls met him at the wooden gate. They stood chatting across the gate for what seemed an age until Moran faced the house with the two envelopes tantalizingly held out. Unable to stand it any longer, Sheila went up to him and before he had time to react seized both envelopes, feverishly tearing open her own and handing the other to Mona, who appeared almost unable to take it. Mona watched Sheila more devour than read the results. Moran was so taken aback by the way Sheila had seized the envelope from his hand that he stood in amazement.

'They're good! They're more than I ever thought . . . Read them.' Without knowing quite what she was doing she thrust them roughly towards Moran.

'Why haven't you even opened yours?' She turned to Mona. She took the letter from her hands and opened it. 'You've done great too,' she hugged her sister and they wheeled one another round on the garden path until the flowerbeds were in danger. Both girls had done well but Sheila had done brilliantly.

'This is great,' Rose said. 'We're very proud.'

Moran, reacting to the exhibition of high spirits, said firmly, 'I think we'll have to consider everything.'

'What do you mean *consider*?' Sheila's voice quavered.

'We'll have to consider where it will all lead to,' he said. 'And what we can afford. Making too much fuss of anything never brings luck.'

But in spite of his words there was a fuss about their success. They had done so well that the convent put photographs of the two girls in the local paper. Moran came back from the post office to tell them that Annie and Lizzie had been singing their praises.

'I told them it was nothing. What else had the girls to do but study? Anybody could do it who got their chance. They nearly beat me,' he said to the whole house, much pleased with what he had said.

The girls looked at him with wide-eyed hurt. They felt that he had let them down in front of others.

'They'll think that you are running down your own children.' Rose articulated what they felt.

'If I was to praise the girls in the post office, being Irish they would *have* to cut them down to size,' Moran argued. 'Since I didn't give them any praise, Annie and Lizzie had to do the praising instead. That way they think twice as much of the girls than if I had praised them myself.' He was very pleased with his own astuteness.

'It would have been better if he had praised us no matter what anyone said,' Sheila said when the girls were alone with Rose, disappointed that he had failed to support them in public no matter what his intentions were.

'Well, that's the way Daddy is,' Rose argued. 'He probably thought that's what would please you most. He's so proud of you all. He thought that he might do you harm if he allowed it to show.'

The solid offer of a place in the Department of Lands came for Mona and a similar job in the Department of Finance for Sheila. The offers came among a number of other lesser positions that the girls had applied for.

'To those that have shall be given too much. To those that have nothing shall be given a kick in the arse,' Moran responded to the luxury of the choices. He assumed both girls would take the civil service jobs. Then a scholarship to university came in for Sheila. Suddenly the whole world was wide open to her.

'I'm saying nothing. I want to stand in nobody's way. She has to make up her own mind. Tonight we'll all have to pray for her guidance,' Moran said.

She played with the choices during the remaining days allowed her, knowing in her heart that she would be forced to take the safe path into the civil service. She went to the convent for advice. Sister Oliver pressed her to grasp her chance and go to university. Sheila argued the hesitations and objections she already felt surrounded by, which were, essentially, Moran's lack of support but the nun pressed her to think about it.

'I was talking to Sister Oliver. She wants me to forget about the civil service and to go to university,' she said as soon as she got home.

'Go to university?' Moran repeated.

'I won the scholarships,' she asserted spiritedly.

'Would the scholarships pay for everything?'

'They'd pay for most of it.'

'Where would the rest come from?'

'I could work during the holidays.' She felt under great pressure.

'What would you study at university?'

'I'd like to do medicine.'

'How long would that take?'

'The most of seven years.'

'Physician heal thyself,' he muttered in a half-overheard aside and went out.

Sheila could not have desired a worse profession. It was the priest and doctor and not the guerrilla fighters who had emerged as the bigwigs in the country Moran had fought for. For his own daughter to lay claim to such a position was an intolerable affront. At least the priest had to pay for his position with celibacy and prayer. The doctor took the full brunt of Moran's resentment.

Sheila withdrew into angry silence. There were moments when she thought of looking for outside help but there was really no one she could turn to. Maggie had barely enough to live on. She considered writing to Luke in London – she had even taken notepaper out – but realized that it would be directly confronting Moran. She could not bring herself to do it.

Throughout, Moran did not attempt to influence Sheila directly but his withdrawal of support was total.

After two days Sheila announced truculently, 'I'm not going to the university. I'll take the civil service.'

'I didn't want to stand in your way, that's why I said nothing but I can't help thinking it is closer to your measure.'

'How?' Her anger brought out his own aggression.

'How, what? How, pig, is it?' he demanded.

'What do you mean, Daddy? I didn't understand what you said, that's all,' she was quick to change but she refused to withdraw.

'You'd understand quick enough if you wanted to. You know

the old saying there's none more deaf than those who do not want to hear.'

'I'm sorry. I just didn't understand, Daddy.'

'Going for medicine is a fairly tall order, isn't it? Even with scholarships it takes money. I consider all my family equal. I don't like to see a single one trying to outdistance another.'

'I didn't say anything like that. I just said what I'd like to do,' she said brokenly, with bitterness.

'That's right. Blame me because the world isn't perfect,' Moran complained equally bitterly. 'Blame, blame. No matter what you do. Blame is all you get in this family.'

Mona stayed out of the turmoil. She was on her certain way into the civil service from the beginning. Full of hidden violence, she was unnaturally acquiescent, fearful that her own unyieldingness would be exposed and its consequences violent.

Once Sheila was securely set towards the civil service as well, as if out of weakness or guilt Moran began courting her with vague, tentative offers; if she were desperate to go to university they could still look into ways of how it could be managed and they would try to manage it somehow no matter how hard it was. She refused. She knew the offers would disappear again the very moment she tried to take them up.

The week before they were going to Dublin he went with the two girls and Rose to Boles in the town.

'You must get what you want. You have to be able to hold your heads as high as anybody else in Dublin. Get the good stuff. The Morans are too poor to afford cheap shoes. There will be money after us when we are gone.' Rose did not take him at his word. She spent carefully. 'You didn't spend half enough when you got the chance,' he said when he saw the bill.

He was plainly suffering because he had denied Sheila her chance of university but he could not have acted in any other way, perhaps through race fear of the poorhouse or plain temperament.

'Don't worry, Daddy,' Mona said. 'You did everything you

could for us. You did far too much.' Sheila nodded in vigorous agreement.

That evening, after Sheila and Mona had left for Dublin, Michael said resentfully, 'They're all gone now.' After Luke and then Maggie had left for London there were still enough people to dull the heartache and emptiness but now that all the girls had gone it was as if the whole house had been cleaned. 'It's not fair.'

'That's life, I'm afraid, Michael,' Rose said.

'How will they fare without us?' his face was soft with tears.

'How will we fare without them?' Rose said. 'They'll manage, please God. We all have to manage somehow.'

'They shouldn't all be gone.'

Moran looked from his son's face to his wife's but his own remained expressionless. When he got up from his chair he was already spilling the beads from their black purse into his palm. 'We'd be better if we'd say our prayers.'

The newspapers were put down, the chairs dragged into place but there was so much space on the floor that the three kneeling figures, Moran erect at the table, Rose and Michael bent at the chairs, looked scattered and far apart. There was an uneasy pause, as if waiting for Mona, at the beginning of the Third Mystery. Moran hurried into the Fourth. Rose too was hesitant as she started the Fifth Mystery. A wind was swirling round the house, sometimes gusting in the chimney, and there was an increasing sense of fear as the trees stirred in the storm outside when the prayers ended. For the first time the house seemed a frail defence against all that beat around it.

The prayers had done nothing to dispel the sense of night and stirring trees outside, the splattering of rain on the glass.

As Moran solemnly replaced his beads in the purse Michael complained again. 'The house feels awful with everybody gone.' Rose looked from Moran to the boy and back again to Moran and held her peace.

'They're gone anyhow,' Moran said. 'They have good jobs. I'll expect they'll be sending us money before long. We'll all be rolling,' Moran said half-jokingly; and as Michael started to sob he touched his thick curly hair. 'They've mollied you for far too long. You'll have to grow up and fight your corner.'

'We'll make tea. There's fruit cake as well as bread and jam. I'm worn out with all the go of the last days,' Rose said.

After Rose and the boy had gone to bed he sat on his own by the raked fire, sitting motionless, staring down at the floor. When he did get up to go to the room he looked like someone who had lost the train of thought he had set out on and had emptied himself into blankness, aware only that he was still somehow present.

Though it was in its late September glory Michael lost all interest in his garden; the falling petals stayed unswept and the flowers wilted and fell into a tangled mess. Several times Rose tried to prod him towards the garden but after a short time he would just stand in it, disheartened, looking on at the disorder before moving away. The girls had praised his green hands. His involvement in the little garden was not strong enough to survive without their praise.

He had few outside interests. He did not play football or any team games nor did he fish or hunt or swim. Knowledge and information he was able to pick up without effort and he always came close to the top of his class without appearing to study. Except for maths he showed no interest in any one subject above another and his liking for mathematics seemed to stem from the fact that it came to him so easily while others struggled. With the girls gone, his main distraction and society had gone, for out of Moran's sight he had loved to tease and play with them and they with him. He was as tall at fifteen as he would ever be and though he would never have Moran's dramatic good looks he was handsome. After his sisters left, he discovered that he was attractive to women but it was to older women that he was drawn. From Moran he inherited a certain contempt for women as well as a dependence on them but it did not diminish his winning ways. The one drawback was his lack of money. To go about with young women he needed money and Moran would not part with any.

He went to Rose. She gave him a little money but grew alarmed when he began to come home late at night. When she got out of bed, anxious to see that he was all right, she discovered that he smelled of drink. At school he began to earn money by doing difficult maths exercises for slower boys. Moran had been listless about the house since the girls had gone but once he discovered that Michael was coming home late at night he acted decisively. Without a word of warning he bolted every door and window in the house and waited up.

When he heard the latch of the back door being raised, he was dozing in darkness. Then he heard various windows being tried. Softly he went to the back door and drew the bolt and as soon as he heard returning footsteps he opened the door.

'This is a nice hour,' he said.

'I was in town. I couldn't get a lift back. I had to walk.'

'What were you doing in town?'

'There was a dance.'

'Did you ask to go to the dance?'

'No.'

'No *what*? No, pig!'

'No, Daddy.'

Moran beckoned him to come in and as he was passing him in the narrow hallway he seized him and struck him violently about the head. 'I'll teach you to come in at this hour! I'll teach you to go places without asking! There must have been drink at this hooley as well!'

Sheltered by his sisters, Michael was unused to any blows and angrily cried out as soon as he was struck. There would have been a violent struggle but for Rose's appearance.

'What an hour to come in at, Michael! You have Daddy up worried about you the whole night.'

'I couldn't get a lift. He hit me,' the boy cried.

'You haven't seen the end of this by half. I'll teach you one good lesson. Nobody's coming into this house at any old hour of the night they like while I'm in charge here.'

'Everybody's tired now. We'll get to bed. Anything that has to be gone into can be gone into in the morning,' Rose said.

Moran glared at her. He seemed about to brush her out of the way to seize the boy but drew back. 'You can thank your lucky stars the woman's here.'

'He hit me,' the boy sobbed.

'And I'll damn well show you what it is to be hit the next time you come into the house at this hour. You're not going to do anything you like while I'm here.'

'I'll go away,' the boy shouted self-pityingly.

'Everybody's tired. Look at the time it is. You can't be coming in at this time. You had poor Daddy and everybody else worried to death about you,' Rose scolded and managed to shepherd both men to their rooms without further trouble.

'I'll see that gentleman in the morning,' Moran warned. 'He needn't think he's getting away with anything in this house.'

Rose got him away to school early in the morning but it was only a postponement. During the weekend Michael had the good sense to stay well in the background and Mona and Sheila came from Dublin for the weekend, which postponed any confrontation further still. Moran was so taken up with the girls and their life in Dublin that he hardly noticed him.

These visits of his daughters from London and Dublin were to flow like relief through the house. They brought distraction, something to look forward to, something to mull over after they had gone. Above all they brought the bracing breath of the outside, an outside Moran refused to accept unless it came from the family. Without it there would have been an ingrown wilting. For the girls the regular comings and goings restored their superior sense of self, a superiority they had received intact from Moran and which was little acknowledged by the wide world in which they had to work and live. That unexamined notion of superiority was often badly shaken and in need of restoration each time they came home. Each time he met them at the station his very presence affirmed and reaffirmed again as he kissed them goodbye. Within the house the outside world was shut out. There was only Moran, their beloved father; within his shadow and the walls of his house they felt that they would never die; and each time they came to Great Meadow they grew again into the wholeness of being the unique and separate Morans.

'That boy thinks he can stroll in here any hour of the day or night he likes. I've warned him once and for all and I'll not warn him again. He may not take heed and if he doesn't I may need your help to bring him to his senses,' Moran confided to Sheila during one of the weekends the girls came from Dublin. She nodded and listened. She did not want to know where the talk led. Tomorrow she would be back in Dublin. 'To bring him once and for all to his senses' was like far-off thunder that could promise any sort of weather.

Moran's warning on the night he locked Michael out had little effect but to make him more calculating. For so many years he had been protected by the cushion of the others that he alone in the house had no residual fear of Moran. When he was going to be late he now made some excuse. Moran was often tired which was reason enough for him not to stay up to check the lateness. But the sorest point was his constant need of money.

'You must think I'm made of money. You must think money grows on bushes. You must think all I have to do is to go out and gather money like a few armfuls of hay for cattle. I had no money at your age. And none of the others in the house ever had the money you want.'

'Everybody at school has money, more money than I ever have,' the boy said resentfully.

'Then their fools of fathers must have more money than sense. I can tell you there's no money here. I can tell you that once and for all and for good.'

Then Michael went to Rose. Again she gave him small sums. She was very fond of the boy, though by now, except for a coltish awkwardness, he was more man in height and strength than boy. All of them now looked forward to Christmas. Each night brought it one day nearer. The girls would be coming home and all of them would be together again under the same roof. Each dull night sharpened that anticipation.

Rose had already made the plum pudding. It lay wrapped in dampened gauze in the biscuit tin on top of the dresser. A week before Christmas Moran dragged a huge red-berried branch through the front door and dumped it in the middle of the room, filling the centre of the floor.

'What's that doing here?' Rose asked in dismay.

'Didn't you tell me to look out for berried holly? You'll not see much redder than that. I don't know how it escaped the birds.'

'I said a few sprigs not a whole tree.'

'Easier to cut the branch than pluck here and there among the thorns. Can't you throw out what you don't want?'

'Oh Daddy, we just want a few bits for the windows and pictures. But the berries are beautiful. It's such a pity to destroy a whole tree for a few sprigs.'

'It'd go to waste on the birds anyway. Better to have too much than too little.' He went out pleased by the mild censure of the tree of red berries lying in the middle of the floor.

It moved Rose to decorate the house at once in order to be rid of the huge branch, and Michael helped. In an hour bits of berried holly were twisted in all the picture cords and left in rows along windowsills and shelves. 'Daddy can never do anything by halves,' Rose laughed as they hauled the branch outside. It still had enough berries to decorate several houses and they both laughed in indulgent amusement.

During these weeks at the prospect of his sisters' homecoming Michael returned to being a child of the house. He was poised on the blurred height, as eager to come down and be cradled and fussed over as to swagger and tomcat it out into the wild. Maggie crossed over to Dublin the night before Christmas Eve. She spent the day in Dublin and the three girls took the late train next day.

Moran left alone for the station. Michael stayed outside the house in the cold clear night until suddenly the lighted squares of the diesel train rattled across the darkness of the Plains. 'The

95

train has passed!' he rushed inside to cry to Rose. In spite of the cold he kept opening the front door. Excited herself, and caught in his excitement, she had not the heart to tell him to keep it closed. 'They're here!' he called to her as soon as the headlights turned into the short avenue, and leaving the door wide open they went to meet the car. By the little wooden gate there were hugs and cries, eager kisses, the calling out of names, Sheila, Maggie, Michael, Mona, Rose, Rose, Rose, Rose, each name an utterance of pleasure and of joy. They were home, they were home for Christmas. Moran's family were all, almost all, under the one roof for Christmas. They had come to what they knew best in the world.

'Look what I brought for Christmas,' Moran laughed proudly when they were all inside. 'Three fine women.' Words rushed against one another from the two who loved to talk, Maggie and Sheila, came to a stop against one another, laughed in impatience at each block, and rushed on. Mona was silent or spoke quietly.

By the time tea was taken everyone was quieter and each of them speaking naturally. All they had to do was observe the happy rituals: help prepare the turkey, remove the curtains from the front windows and light a single candle in each window, kneel to say the Rosary together, dress and get ready to go to midnight Mass. As they knelt on the floor, Moran began, 'In the name of the Father and of the Son and of the Holy Ghost we offer up this most holy Rosary for the one member of the family who is absent from the house tonight,' and the dramatizing of the exception drew uncomfortable attention to the disturbing bonds of their togetherness.

The three girls, Rose and Michael packed into the small car which Moran was driving to midnight Mass. They sat on one another's knees and joked. 'I think you've put on weight since you went to Dublin.' 'Your knees haven't got softer anyhow since,' laughing and chattering away the discomfort of the physical constraint. Single candles burned in the windows of all the houses they passed and pinpoints of light glittered as far as the first slopes of the mountain in the sea of darkness.

Once they crossed the bridge the church appeared like an enormous lighted ship in the night. There was something wonderful and moving about leaving the car by the roadside and walking together in the cold and darkness towards the great lighted church. The girls clasped hands in silence and drew closer together as they walked. Once they passed through the church gates several people came over to them to welcome them home and to wish them a happy Christmas, whispering how well they looked as they bowed away with little nods and smiles. The church itself was crowded and humming with excitement. There were many others like the Moran girls who had come home for Christmas. They would all be singled out as they came away from the altar rail after Communion and discussed over hundreds of dinners the next day: who was home and where they were living and what they worked at and how they looked and who they got their looks from and what they wore last night as they came away from the rail. As good-looking girls in their first flowering, the three Morans were among the stars of the Communion rail that Christmas night.

'I'll leave you to this cackle,' Moran said indulgently as soon as he finished his cup of tea after they got back to the house. 'But my advice is to go to bed.'

'I suppose we should all go to bed,' Sheila said vigorously as soon as Moran had left but no sooner had she said the words than she launched into, 'And did you see Mary Fahey?' which led on to more people and clothes and positions and looks, until Rose said with her apologetic little laugh, 'We could go on like this the whole night and Daddy will wonder what on earth we were talking about all this time.'

When she was gone, the heart of the talk was broken; and then to Sheila's 'I suppose we should go to bed', they went.

Because of midnight Mass the whole house was able to sleep late. Once they rose the day was set. There would be no surprises, pleasant or unpleasant. No visits would be made or received this day – it was considered to be improper to leave one's own house on Christmas Day – and the day would climb to the glory of the feast of turkey and stuffing and then slip back again to night in card playing.

'I suppose there's not much use inquiring about that brother of yours,' Moran asked awkwardly. 'Anybody normal would be with his own family at Christmas.' It was as if he wanted to get all unpleasantness out of the way early in deference to the day and feast.

'I didn't see him very much. He lives the other side of London. It takes over an hour to get there on the tube,' Maggie said carefully.

'What's he doing with himself for Christmas?'

'He said he was going down to Kent. He has friends there.'

'What kind of friends?'

'People he works with.'

'Has he got himself a decent job then?'

'He's started a business with people he got to know. They buy old houses. He says he has to spend too much time in the office now. He'd sooner be out and around the sites.'

'That'll all blow up in his face one of these days. You have to depend on too many people. There are plenty of rogues about but of course you can't tell that gentleman anything.'

'He doesn't talk much about it.'

'He'd be afraid I'd hear too much. How does he look himself?'

'He looks much the same as he always did.'

'Well, I'm glad you go to the trouble of seeing him even if he doesn't act as if he's still a member of my family. All the members of my family are equal even if they think otherwise. They should never be looked down on or excluded. Not even if they want to exclude themselves.'

The room was already full of delicious smells. Two tables were put together out from the window and covered with a white cloth. The places were set. The huge browned turkey was placed in the centre of the table. The golden stuffing was spooned from its breast, white dry breadcrumbs spiced with onion and parsley and pepper. There were small roast potatoes and peas and afterwards the moist brandy-soaked plum pudding. Brown lemonade was squirted into the glasses from syphons with silver tops.

'I'm so hungry I could eat a young child,' Moran said and everybody laughed. He sat at the head of the elongated table. Before Rose came he always ate alone at the big table. The meal was ringed by the Grace he recited before and after.

Then, after the washing-up and tidying, it was a slow struggle to get through what remained of the day. Mona and Sheila read. The others played the long card game of Twenty-one for penny stakes. Moran won the most. There were stifled yawns while tea was made after cards and Moran made loud and exaggerated yawns for comic effect. The whole house was glad to slip away early to bed after the Rosary was said.

As if to make up for the sealing of the house on Christmas Day all doors were thrown wide open on St Stephen's Day. People continually trooped between houses, bringing presents or friendly words or just making calls. Not many visitors ever called to Moran's house but the girls were fêted everywhere they called to. 'You're home! You're home for Christmas!' and hands were gripped and held instead of shaken to show the strength of feeling. Michael went with the girls to some of the houses but had to travel very much in their shadow. Tired of being ignored he went home with ill-grace to Rose. They both went to the door together whenever the wren-boys knocked, local children in gaudy carnival rags wearing masks or warpaint. Few could dance or sing or play properly. Usually they performed a painful parody of all three while they rattled coins vigorously about in a tin canister. Michael lost his grievance as he began to enjoy their incompetence while trying to identify the children underneath their colourful disguises. Between the motley bands of children, the real wren-boys came on the Arigna coal lorry. The girls made sure that they were in the house. Many of the wren-boys did not bother to wear disguises. An accordion struck up as they swarmed from the lorry, then more accordions, fiddles, fifes and a drum. Dancers skipped up the path and caught Rose and the girls and danced them round the room in perfect time. There were screeches of laughter and provocative cheers to the music. Everyone went silent when an old song was sung in a pure tenor with bare accompaniment; then more music and dancing and clowning. Moran liked the traditional music and handed them a larger sum than usual. Before the Ardcarnes left they urged everyone to come to the big dance in the barn that night. As usual all the money they lifted would be spent on whiskey and porter and lemonade and sandwiches and cake and tea. The same musicians would play. All would drink and eat and dance. The little party ended as suddenly as it began with murmurs and clear words of thanks and warnings of *Don't let us miss you tonight*; and then the melancholy sounds of the instruments being packed.

Rose and the girls tried to prevail on Moran to go with them to the wren-boys' dance in the barn that night but the one time he had gone with Rose had been more than enough. 'There's a time for dancing and a time for being out of sight. Why don't you go with the girls?' he said to Rose.

'You know I'll not go unless you go, Daddy,' Rose said. 'You know there will be people far older than us there.'

'That's their business,' Moran said and shuffled out of the room.

In their excitement all the girls looked beautiful dressed for the dance but none was more excited or more carefully dressed than Michael. The girls hardly noticed him. Though tall he was reed-like and they still looked on him as a child. Moran drove them to the dance. They would walk or get a lift home: there was the unspoken sexual excitement of meeting someone who would see them home.

There were no lights around the gates and shuttered gate-house when they drove up the narrow avenue. They found the big house in darkness but round the back among the sheds the enormous barn was all lit up by lines of naked electric bulbs strung up on poles. Inside, it was already full. Three musicians who had come on the Arigna lorry to the house earlier in the day played reels on a platform of raised planks but no one was dancing yet. Girls were drinking tea and talking in groups at trestle tables set around the walls. Older women drank whiskey with men their age. Around the porter barrels stood crowds of young men. It hardly changed from year to year and could have been the same scene as Rose and Moran had walked in on.

At once Michael joined one of the crowds and took a glass of stout. None of the Moran girls drank. They were as much shocked by the confidence with which Michael moved about among the men as by his actual drinking. Their little brother had grown up without their noticing. He moved loudly among the men as the alcohol went to his head. The men merely turned their backs on the boy's show of masculinity. Catching his sisters' stares of disapproval, he waved his glass to them across the floor and started to survey the women.

He was not a good dancer but he moved and held himself well as his father had done on such barn floors and he gave Nell Morahan his whole attention. Defiantly, when the dance ended, he took her across to the table that had whiskey and stout. In the same spirit she asked for whiskey. To the Moran girls this was shameless, even wanton. She did not care. She knew that they considered themselves above the Morahans of the Plains. She held their baby brother in her experienced hands. He did not flinch from their disapproving stares but, laughing, toasted them in whiskey across the floor. They were forced to turn away into a closed circle.

Nell Morahan came from a small farm on the high part of the Plains. Her father, Frank Morahan, worked as a day labourer for big farmers all the year round, leaving his family to manage his own poor acres, helping as much as he could on Sundays and long evenings. They were looked down on. None of the children was clever; there was no escape through the schools. Nell went to work as a maid for a solicitor's family in the town, where she had her first taste of sexual fondling with the sons of the house home on holidays from college, fondling she had no aversion to. Next she went as a shop girl to a small town near Dublin and had a string of boyfriends from the terraces, when an aunt brought her to New York. There, she showed the family trait of a willingness to work, first in an ice-cream factory, next in a dry-cleaning place and finally as a waitress, where she found that her good humour and energy could earn her more in a week than she could save in a year in Ireland. She had lived with an older man but felt used when he showed no sign of keeping promises. In her practical way she left him without much regret or hurt. Now she was twenty-two and home for a few months with money of her own. She had bought clothes and shoes for her brothers and sisters and other useful things for the cottage on the Plains. For herself she bought a small car that she intended to leave with the family. She would take a younger sister with her when she went back to New York. Above all she was determined to show her father a good time and to have a bit of a fling for herself on the side. She was as far from ugliness as she was from beauty and she was young and strong and spirited. Michael Moran was only fifteen but he had good looks and sexual charm. All through her childhood she felt that farms like the Morans' had a richness and greenness in spite of her father's tired assertions to the contrary. When Michael crossed the barn floor to ask Nell Morahan to dance it was natural that they should go together.

'You'd think she'd have more to do than cradle snatch,' Maggie said furiously.

'All I hope is that it doesn't get to Daddy's ears,' Sheila said. The closed, angry circle could only be broken by men crossing the floor to ask them to dance. During the next dances he clowned around the floor. His sisters tried to ignore them but later when they looked for the couple again they were missing from the barn. Though each of the girls had many offers during the dances from men wanting to see them home, they left alone and together. After the last dance had been played and the tired musicians were preparing to play the National Anthem, only Sheila was aggressive enough to cross the floor and ask Michael, 'Are you coming home with us?'

'No, I have my own lift. You know Nell Morahan?' Instead of taking her hand Sheila nodded curtly and marched away.

'What's the matter with her?'

'You've stolen her little brother,' he answered and called after his sisters, 'Don't forget to leave the back door open,' as they left in a tight knot of indignation, pursued by his laughter.

Nell's car was parked on the avenue. It was black and sleek and inside it smelled of new leather. Two sisters of Nell's and her brother sat in the back, Michael with Nell in front. He was fifteen years of age and commanded the world.

As he chattered to the passengers in the back, she drove to their cottage in the Plains in silence and as she dropped them off she called, 'I'll not be long. I'm just leaving Michael home.' Before she reached the yew tree at the gate she turned up a disused lane and switched off the lights. Already his hand was moving between her thighs as she drove. When she turned to him he came to her too eagerly but soon his young straining body was being steered to do as she wanted and no more. When he reached the first luxuriant peace, she made it seem as if he had reached it all on his own, tousling his hair, saying, 'You smell lovely. Your skin is so soft,' and kissing him over and over.

The back door had been left unlatched. When he came in, the house was dark and silent. Holding his shoes he went without making a sound to his room. But in the morning he had to face his sisters' furious resentment. Openly and not a little proudly he met their anger. They could not take him for a child any more. Nonchalantly he ate his breakfast as they scolded. There was nothing they could do. They could not risk telling Moran. The very enclosedness of the house ensured that Moran would not hear about it in any other way. When the girls told Rose, she laughed heartily.

'Well, didn't poor Michael fall on his feet. Who'd ever think it?'

'Look at their ages. We'll be nothing but a laughing stock,' they said angrily.

'In a few months there will not be a word about it. Nell will go back to America and that will be that; but don't bother Daddy with a word,' she counselled.

'Daddy would soon put manners on the brat.'

The full resentment turned on Nell Morahan and she kept

out of their way. The sisters went only to the local dances. Nell drove with Michael to Longford where they were not known.

In a week the Christmas holidays were over. The girls went back to work. The house felt empty again. The schools opened.

Rose called Michael as she had called him on every school morning since she had come to the house and gave him breakfast.

'You seem a little tired this morning, Michael,' Rose teased, but all he was able to do in response was to rub his eyes.

He set off for school that morning as usual but he never went to school again. Nell met him in the car at the edge of the town and they drove to the ocean at Strandhill. When they parked at the old cannon on its wooden carriage there wasn't another car in sight. 'In summer it's jammed,' he said. The tide was far out below the rocks but the waves were mountainous, and white rain blinded the windscreen when the wipers stopped. Nell switched them on again. Crosswinds rocked the car. He found it all exciting and told Nell how good it was compared to the summers Moran had taken a cottage for a fortnight and they had all come here. 'God, it was boring.'

'How could it be boring by the sea? We always had to work in the fields in the summer,' she said.

'It was because *he* was here,' he laughed uproariously at what he imagined was wit; and then, growing bored, he reached for her. She kissed him and then pushed him away playfully but firmly.

'It's no good for me in the morning,' she said.

He sat sullenly away from her staring out through the semicircle the wipers made on the windscreen at the wild ocean and the long strand, the strand on which he had watched the same ocean encircle and wash away a sand castle he had made with bucket and spade not so many summers before. To Nell's annoyance he put his feet up on the dashboard and would not take them down. As quickly as the rain had come the sky cleared and it became a different day. A weak sun shone out on the water. They left the car and climbed down over the blackened boulders to the strand. The wind, blowing the whole length of the level strand, tugged at their hair and clothes. He played and romped around her, tried to walk backwards into the wind until he nearly fell over, and then seized her hand and they both tried to run against the wind. The closer they got to the shelter of the Point the easier it was to walk. Suddenly at the Point itself they were in the shelter of the high dunes at the edge of the golf links and it was like looking back from a still room at all the turbulence of sea and wind they had waded through. This time when he reached for her she came into his arms. Her hair and face tasted of sea spray. Awkwardly they climbed together away from the calm strand, using the coarse tussocks to pull themselves up the slopes of the dunes, their shoes filling with the damp sand as they walked. In a hollow between high dunes they spread out raincoats on the sand and kicked away their shoes. She then, half-kneeling, pulled away her underthings and moved close to him for warmth. He pulled down his clothes over his thighs and entered her as she had shown him on their first night, very gently and a little timidly, in spite of the terrible urging of his need. Above them the wind whipped only at the highest tussocks and the ocean sounded far away. When he entered her for the third time she was ready to search for her own pleasure and he was now able to wait. Such was her strength that he was frightened. She shouted, seized him roughly at the hips, and forced him to move; and when it was over she opened her eyes and with her hands held his face for a quick, grateful kiss he couldn't comprehend. The weak sun stood high above them. Feeling the damp cold, they dressed, shook the sand out of their shoes and raincoats and climbed back down to the shore. There was not even a dog chasing a stick along the whole empty strand, only several birds walking sedately along the tideline which had now come much further up on the beach. As if they had set out on a journey they felt morally bound to complete, they walked the whole way back past the cannon as far as the ruined church on the opposite point. For all his bravado Michael was full of anxiety. He would still have to go back to Moran with the schoolboy's bundle of books in a few hours no matter what the glory was of his first-found manhood. Nell by his side had her own worries. In a few weeks she would be back in the Bronx. Michael was too young. You should take what you have while you can, plain country sense told her, but it was not so simple. She always wanted more. The whole empty strand of Strandhill was all around them and they had the whole day. There is nothing more difficult to seize than the day.

'Do you think it's safe?' he asked.

'That's just like a man to ask now,' Nell said. 'You have nothing to worry about.'

They picked dilsk from the rocks below the roofless church and examined several clear pools between the rocks. There was much minuscule life in the pools but no stranded fish.

'I don't understand what you mean when you say it was boring here. Wasn't it a change?'

'God,' he said. 'You should have been here. He brought a lorry load of turf here to pay for the rent. We had to sell it from door to door. There was no danger of *him* going door to door selling.'

'That wouldn't be a big deal when you're little.'

'It was horrible going round the houses,' he betrayed the same sense of separateness the father had instilled in the others, which was plainly less than useful when it came to selling turf. 'You'd feel like crawling into a hole.'

To get back to the car they had to face into the wind again. They were hungry. All the places along the seafront were closed for the winter and so they drove to Sligo. In Castle Street they found a plain café and had hamburgers and bread and chips with a pot of scalding tea. Then, tired, they wandered around the town. They would have liked to have gone to the Gaiety to see a western with Alan Ladd but they hadn't time enough. He was very quiet as they drove back and she left him a few miles from the house. Bravely he waved to her as she drove away.

'How was school?' Rose called as soon as he came in.

'Just the same as ever,' he answered. He had a habit of switching into his own thoughts while giving the appearance of listening but this evening he followed every syllable of Rose's good-humoured account of her day.

'Now eat your dinner, Michael.'

He gathered that they hadn't heard he had missed school. 'Thanks, Rose.'

After a while Moran came in but he didn't want to talk. A few times he threw a glance in his son's direction but the boy stayed hidden in a book.

'I want you to give a hand with some sheep,' he said as he rose to go out.

'When would suit you, Daddy?'

'Now.'

Moran and the dog had already run the sheep into the yard where they were huddled together, wide-eyed with fear. When Moran and Michael came into the yard they set off in a wild panic until they huddled at bay in another corner.

'They're so stupid,' Michael laughed like a child at their panic.

'They're like some people,' Moran responded tersely.

Michael measured the drench into a small bottle. Moran forced it down the sheeps' throats while Michael held them. Then they turned the sheep on their backs and pared and bathed the small hooves. When they were finished they marked each one with a dab of blue paint before letting it free. There were more than sixty sheep to do and it was slow and monotonous. Michael grew bored and started to make mistakes. Moran almost hit him when he allowed a startled sheep to break loose, knocking Moran aside; and then he dropped the can of drench.

'God, O God, O God. If I could only do this on my own. You can't pay attention for a minute, can't watch for a minute what you are doing,' Moran seized the can violently and poured the measure himself.

'I didn't ask to do this,' the boy cried with equal violence.

'Of course you didn't ask to do any of this. All you'd ever ask to do is sit on your arse and entertain women.'

'I was doing the best I could. I couldn't help that the can slipped,' Michael countered.

'Are we going to go on or are you going to whinge all day?' Moran asked and resentfully they went back to working together again. When it was done Moran watched the sheep quietly stream out of the yard. They wouldn't have to be touched for another two months. He turned in gratitude to thank the boy. He had forgotten how good two people could be working together. A man working alone was nothing. If the boy wanted to come in with him the two of them could do anything. They could run this place like clockwork. They could in time even take over other farms, a dream he had once had about his eldest son: together they could take over everything.

Michael had gone into the house without asking Moran's leave. Bitterly he closed the field gate on the sheep. Then he checked that the cattle were tended for the night. When he came in he found Michael changed and standing confidently in front of the fire.

'You were fairly quick away,' Moran said. 'I turned round to say something to you as I was letting out the sheep and there was no longer sight or light.'

'I thought we were finished.'

'You might have asked.'

'I didn't think there was any need. I thought we were finished.'

'It'd be natural manners but I don't imagine there'd be any use expecting anything like manners round this place,' Moran said.

Outside the window the fields were darkening rapidly. Rose bustled reproachfully round Michael at the fire and he moved away to the table. Demonstratively he had books and writing materials out on the table.

'I've warm socks for you here, Daddy. There's a change of underwear in the hot press. You'll feel better once you get out of the old duds.'

Moran took off his wellingtons and sat in the big car chair in his stockinged feet. He stirred when she spoke but continued staring vacantly out into the empty space of the room and didn't

108

answer. 'Who cares anyhow?' he muttered to himself. 'Who cares? Who cares anyhow?'

Though they had just spent the day together, Michael and Nell arranged to meet again that night. She would wait for him in the car at the Rockingham gates. Michael could not leave the house until the Rosary was said. He chaffed while he waited but there was nothing he could do. To leave the house before prayers were said would invite certain confrontation. This night Rose had to remind Moran that the prayers had not yet been said. By the time he put the newspaper down on the cement and dropped to his knees at the table Nell was already sitting in her car outside the big gateway. Michael suffered keenly the incongruity of his position – a man with a woman by the sea in the early day and now a boy on his knees on the floor. When it came to his turn to recite the Third Decade he gave it out stridently. The tone drew a sharp glance from Moran but he did not intercept the prayers. He waited until he had risen from his knees to say, 'That was a peculiar way you had of giving out your Decade.' Violence between the man and the youth was just a flint-spark away. 'To my poor ears it showed a certain lack of respect.'

'I meant no disrespect,' Michael backed away.

'I'm very glad to hear it. People who get too hot under the collar generally get a cooling.'

Michael didn't answer. He didn't even risk saying that he was going out. He slipped outside, taking his coat on the way and pulling it on in the darkness while he ran to the gates. Though he was over an hour late Nell was still waiting in the car when he reached the gates.

The next morning they drove again to Sligo. This time they saw the western at the early matinée in the Gaiety. During the following weeks they drove to every place around they ever wanted to see, even as far as Galway. They drove to Mullingar and Longford. In Ballymote they stood together in front of every shop window in the town. On a clear Thursday they crossed the border and walked hand in hand between the long rows of stalls in Enniskillen. Beside the gates of the mart she bought him a cheap wristwatch from an Indian stall. He had never owned a watch of his own before. Though it was winter they drove many times to the ocean, to Rosses Point and Mullaghmore and Bundoran as well as to the wild strand at Strandhill. He arrived back each time with his books to Rose and Moran just as it was starting to get dark.

Sheila and Mona came from Dublin for the weekend. This time Michael hid rather than flaunted what was going on. They were suspicious of him but they had to be back at their office desks on Monday and hadn't time enough to find out. Moran's isolation meant that no one had come to him and no one was going to risk letting anything slip to Rose when she went to the shops.

For Nell these weeks were the best of her life, weeks she would look back on as a lost happiness she had strayed into at the wren-boys' dance in the barn. Yet somehow, mysteriously, it had slipped out of her grasp. Throughout the affair she was the more responsible of the two. That she had never gone to school a day longer than the legal requirement and had worked all her life with her hands made her value education more than those to whom it was open. 'Are you sure you're not ruining everything by skipping school like this?'

'I'm finished with school. I'm not going back. This has nothing to do with it.' The fiercest urge was to break out of his life as it was. He could not endure his life in the house any longer. By going the way he was going the crisis was certain to come from without. By doing what he was doing he was certain to bring it on. Not until then would it have to be faced.

'You'll never get the chance of school again,' she said.

'You'll never get anything again,' he responded bitterly.

'What will you do then?'

'Maybe I could go back to America with you?'

She looked at his childish egotism and innocence and bent towards him in a wildness of wishing; but her commonsense told her that it could never be, that all the world was against it.

'You'd not find it easy in America,' she said.

'I'd manage,' he laughed confidently. 'If we can't go to America why don't we drive to Sligo?'

They spent all of the next day in Sligo but their days together were running out. Nell's money was almost gone. She began to feel a little guilty that she had spent so much of her time and money on Michael instead of on her own family though he was not hard on money and any bits of money of his own he got his hands on he spent it all on her.

'I'll have to be going soon, Michael,' she said to him one night as they sat in the car watching a white moon above Lough Key casting a bright roadway on the choppy waters.

Without warning he began to cry, not sure whether he was crying for his own loss or for Nell, having to leave this quiet place and face back to the uncaring world of America. She took him in her arms, cradling him, brushing back his hair until he turned towards her.

'You should go back to school,' she told him. 'That way you'll have a better job later on in your life.'

'No,' he said. 'I'm finished with school.'

'What'll you do?'

'Maybe I could go out to you in America before long?' he asked again. It fell with such a sweetness that she did not want to question further or to see or think what they were doing beyond this hour or if they were doing anything at all.

If he was waiting for his mind to be made up for him by provoking action from without, it came with alarming speed the following evening. Nell and he had crossed the border to Enniskillen for the Thursday market that morning. He had come home as usual with his books around six. Moran was seated very still in the car chair. Rose was bustling round the house. There was no place set for his meal at the table. Before a word was spoken he sensed that he was in danger.

'We had a visitor today,' Moran said.

'Who?'

'Relax,' Moran said sarcastically. 'Your friend Brother Michael from the school. He came out to inquire about you. He thought you were sick. It seems you've not been seen in school since Christmas.'

'I wasn't able to go to school any more,' he began to cry.

'And why, may I inquire?'

'I couldn't face it any more.'

'We are surprised at you, Michael,' Rose said.

'How did you spend your time?'

'I just stayed away.'

'Where did you go?'

'Just here and there.'

'Where's here-and-there? I never heard of it.'

'Around the town, just here and there.' He felt cornered.

'You try to lie and bluff as well! I made a few inquiries after the Brother went. I discovered Miss Morahan that's home from America has been chauffeuring you round the entire country.'

There was no point in any further answers.

'I don't know why you did it to us, Michael,' Rose said.

'Rose and myself feed you, give you a roof above your head, send you to school and that's the thanks we get.'

Michael was silent. The pauses between the sobs were longer.

'You have nothing to say. You're not even sorry.'

'I'm sorry,' he sniffed.

'I'm afraid you'll have to be taught a lesson as well. I want you to go to your room, take off your clothes and I'll see you there in a few minutes. Maybe we can still sort this business out just between the two of us.' So quiet and authoritative was Moran's voice that Michael actually moved to go to the room; suddenly he realized what he was being asked to do and stopped.

'No!' the boy shouted in fear and outrage.

'You'll do what I say if you want to stay on in this house.' Moran moved with great quickness from the chair but the boy was too strong. He easily parried his father's lunge and ran from the house.

'He'll have to come back,' Moran breathed heavily. 'And when he does that gentleman will have to be taken within one inch of his life.'

112

He did not think of going back. He walked all the way to Morahan's, high on the Plains. The car was outside their asbestos-roofed cottage. A younger sister of Nell's came to the door and asked him in.

'No, thanks, Brigid,' he flashed a wan smile. 'I want to see Nell.' And when she came to the door he said, 'He found out about the school. He was like a madman. He could kill someone. I ran away.'

'Are you going to go back?'

'I'm going to England,' he said decisively. 'If I could get to Dublin the crowd there would give me the fare. I wonder if you'd loan me the money for the train.'

'When does it go?'

'In the morning.'

'Where will you stay till then?'

'I'll find somewhere, some shed or some place,' he said dramatically.

'Are you sure you want to go like this?'

'I'll hitch if you can't give me the fare.'

'I'll drive you to Dublin,' she said. 'Won't you come into the house while I'm getting ready?'

'I don't want to face into the house the way I am.'

'You better sit in the car.'

He sat in the car and played the radio, fiddling with the knobs. Fits of rage and fear would shake him every time he thought of Moran, then change to self-pity. By the time Nell came he was tired of playing the radio. She was dressed up and carried a suitcase which she put in the back of the car.

They drove past the house and school, through Longford and Mullingar, towns they had been happy in for whole days. Now only the bars were open, the lighted streets wintry and empty, the silent rows of parked cars funereal along the sidewalk.

'He told me to go to the room. He told me to take off all my clothes and wait for him in the room. I ran out of the house.'

'He must be crazy.'

'Once he made Luke take off all his clothes in the room. We heard the sound of the beating.'

113

'Would Luke help you if you got to London?'

'I know he would. Luke always did whatever he said he would do.'

'There's no use going to your sisters at this hour. We might as well stay the night in a hotel. I'll get you to your sisters early in the morning.'

'Would they let us stay the night in a hotel?'

'As long as it is a *big* hotel they won't mind,' she laughed. 'As long as we can pay.'

'Are you sure it won't be too much?'

'Next week I'll be in America,' she said.

'I'll write to you,' he said and she just pressed his knee as she drove through Enfield. After Maynooth she told him to watch out for hotels. On the outskirts of the city the West Country looked large and nondescript and they had vacancies. Accentuating her American accent she paid in cash and the girl in reception hardly looked at them as they filled the forms and were handed the room keys. The room was plain but comfortable. As soon as they saw the room they both realized how ravenous they were. Downstairs the dining room was empty but still open. 'We might as well treat ourselves this evening.' Nell encouraged him to pick whatever he wanted from the menu. She had steak, he an enormous mixed grill with chips. They had to wait longer for the food to be served in the empty dining room than it took them to eat. Unused to such places, Michael spoke in whispers. Only when he laughed did his voice ring out.

All through the night they made love. The anxiety of his years soon gave way to tenderness and great gratitude. Each time that she thought he was at last slipping into sleep he would come into her again. She received him as if he were both man and child, his slenderness cancelled by strength, his unsureness by pride; and she took him too each time as if she were saying a slow and careful farewell to a youth she herself had to work too hard ever to have had when she was young. Not until morning did they fall into a sleep of pure exhaustion

114

and as soon as she woke she roused him and drove him to the part of the city where his sisters lived.

'I'll write,' he said in the empty morning street.

'You have the address?'

'I have.' He tapped his jacket.

'I'll write as well.'

'You'll see me in New York.' He rapped the hollow roof of the car with his fist as a signal of affection before the car moved away.

The whole street appeared to be sleeping. A milkman delivered bottles to doorsteps from an electric float, the motor whirring when it moved. He was a long time knocking before there was any sound at all within the house where Sheila and Mona lived. Then an upstairs window opened. Mona leaned out in her nightclothes. Her surprise vied with total disbelief.

'What are *you* doing here?' she demanded.

'I ran away,' he said.

'What are you coming here for?'

'I'm going to England.'

'I'll come down,' she said and closed the window.

He heard her speak rapidly to someone in the room, probably Sheila. It seemed a very long time before anyone came to the door. They were both dressed when the door opened.

'How did you get this far?' Sheila demanded.

'I hitched.'

'In the middle of the night?'

'I got several small lifts and then a milk lorry took me in this morning.' He told them the story of how he ran away much as he had told Nell but he did not mention her at all. 'He told me to go to the room and take off my clothes and wait for him there.'

'He'll kill us if we give you the fare.'

'I'll have to get it somehow. I'm not going home.'

They fried sausages and eggs and bacon, made him tea and toast. The man and woman who owned the house came down and were told the story. The man was quiet and wore his postman's uniform. In spite of their fear both girls were begin-

115

ning to get caught up in the excitement of the drama and when they went to work Sheila took Michael with her into the Kildare Street offices. There the excitement continued. Before long the whole building seemed to have called in on Sheila. A young man, polite and good-looking, was running away from home. To grey civil servants it brought back the glow of their own youth. If it were not for the obligatory procedures that had to be adhered to, he would probably have been offered a civil service position there and then. 'It's terrible. We don't know what to do,' Sheila kept repeating but she was enjoying the stir and the attention.

In her secretive way she had already made up her mind how she was going to take care of the situation but she continued to seek counsel which was drawing sympathy her way. She had a boyfriend now, a civil servant like herself, and Mona and he joined them for lunch in the huge canteen. Michael was having a fine time. Here were people and excitement and noise and bustle. Gone was the oppression of Moran's house. His charm would work here as well as anywhere. But Sheila had different plans. 'You can't go to England,' she said.

'Why? I'm not going home.'

'You haven't finished school. If you finish school you can go anywhere. If you leave now you can be nothing but a labourer for the rest of your life.'

She ignored his protests that it was his own business. She was going to see Moran and Rose that evening. If Moran wouldn't agree to take him back he could stay in Dublin with them. He had only another couple of years to do after which he would have all the choices he wanted, even labouring if that was what he wanted to do. The way he was going about it he would have no choices.

She took the train to Great Meadow to face Moran. So much time had passed without news of Michael that they had grown anxious and were relieved to see her. Moran had no reason to imagine that she might not be completely on his side in the matter.

'So he ran to you,' Moran said.

'He hitched.'

'I have a plan for that boy,' Moran said.

It was simple. They would bring Michael home and the whole house would help supervise a beating that Moran would administer. That way it would be properly done and they would be legally protected; besides, Moran was not strong enough any more to handle him on his own: 'So he'll be taught a lesson he'll never forget for the rest of his life.'

'He'd not come home for us. The only way he'll come home and go back to school is if everything can be forgotten.'

'There'd be no need to tell him.'

'I'd have to tell him,' Sheila said doggedly.

'Of course I have no right to expect any consideration in this house,' Moran shouted; but there was little he could do.

Sheila went back to Dublin and she and Mona brought Michael down a few days later. They had to promise him that if there was trouble again they would give him every help to stay in Dublin or to go to London.

'Do your best,' they urged him. 'If it doesn't work out we'll give you every help. Two more years you'll be finished school and you can go anywhere you want.'

When he entered the house it was with extreme watchfulness and a self-conscious sheepishness that was almost comic.

'You're welcome,' a grieved Moran looked away as he put out his hand to him. 'All my family are always welcome back to this house, without exceptions.'

Sheila's boyfriend, Sean Flynn, had driven them all down. He attracted most of Moran's attention who assumed she would not have drawn him into a family situation as delicate as the present one if she did not intend to marry him. Sean Flynn was flattered; he was used to pleasing. They talked about politics, the land the Flynns farmed in Clare, his huge family and they both agreed that the family was the basis of all society and every civilization. Moran enjoyed himself and felt cheated when the time came for them to head back for Dublin.

'The next time you must come for a proper visit,' Moran said as he shook his hand by the car.

'If I'm asked,' Sean Flynn turned to tease Sheila.

'You'll be asked,' Moran laughed. 'You should never give these women too much sway. They'd have you in leg-irons before you'd know.'

It seemed that Sean Flynn had won her father's approval. 'That'll do now,' Sheila said, hiding her confusion and pleasure by arranging things in the back of the car.

Michael was pale and apprehensive in the house but Moran did not as much as look at him.

'That Sean Flynn seems an intelligent, well brought up young man,' Moran said as he took out his beads for the Rosary.

'I'm glad for Sheila,' Rose said. 'She needs someone quiet.'

'Your bed is aired,' she said very gently to Michael after the prayers were said. 'I'm sure you must be worn out.'

'I think I'll go to bed then,' the boy said. He didn't know whether to slip away or to go up to his father as usual and try to kiss him good night.

'Go up and kiss Daddy,' Rose whispered when she saw him hesitate.

Moran held up his face to be kissed. His eyes were almost closed. The whole aspect was one of invoking some higher power to help him fulfil his fatherly duty. The boy touched the stubble more than the lips before backing away.

'Good night, Daddy.'

'Good night, son. God bless you.'

The very next day he had to face back into school. He was welcomed by the Brothers as if he had come back after a very long illness, for Sheila had called at the monastery on her way to Dublin and blamed his absence on some difficulty at home.

'You know yourself that you have one of the best heads in the whole school,' Brother Superior Gerald flattered him gently. 'If you get down to study now you can do anything. You'll have the whole world before you. But if you throw in the towel you'll be nothing.'

The words were like an old refrain that he was sick of. The new attention, even adulation, from the other boys he found irksome. He could not endure the school – filing into classrooms, listening to arid words, watching meaningless diagrams chalked on the blackboard: it was as if everything was specially designed to drive him crazy. He knew he could not go on like this. Nell had gone. All his life seemed to be elsewhere.

On the road her blue car passed him. One of the younger Morahans was driving. They waved but made no effort to stop. Alone, he cried out and cursed. The small alder and sally trees along the road, the brown clumps of dead rushes down to the flood waters of Drumharlow did not appear to bow in the friendly way of long familiarity. They were just bushes; worse than hostile, they were useless. He could not stay. He could not go away. Without any definite plan he would act in such a way that they would be forced to drive him away.

That evening Michael dropped the deferential air he had always worn in front of Moran. He was not openly impolite but withdrawn and heavy. Moran was irritated by the conduct, watched carefully but held his peace. This went on for several days. School continued to be intolerable. His schoolfellows found him self-absorbed and violent when he joined in games. They ignored him. In a dull fog of self-pity he went in and out of class. In the house each day grew more tense. Rose was on edge. All she could do was to try bouts of amiable prattling that drew no response from either father or son. The very air felt as if it was being so stretched out that it had to change or break: as small a thing as a salt cruet eventually brought all that was between them to a head.

'That salt,' Moran demanded.

'What salt?'

'Are there two salts? Pass that salt!'

Instead of lifting the small cruet, Michael pushed it across the table towards his father. Moran seethed as he watched. As it was pushed, the small glass cruet touched a fold in the tablecloth and overturned.

'You wouldn't pass salt that way to a dog,' Moran rose from the table. 'Have you any idea who you are passing that salt to?'

'I didn't mean for it to overturn.' Michael was at an intolerable disadvantage sitting down.

'You just shoved it over to the dog.'

'I tell you I didn't mean . . .'

'I'll teach you to mean something!' Moran struck him violently but he managed partly to avert the blow, the chair falling over as he jumped to his feet. 'You needn't think you're going to Lord-Muck-it round here for the rest of your days.'

The second blow he took on the arms but it still forced him to back against the sewing machine. He felt the metal against his back but no injury or fear. Using the old foot machine as a springboard he jumped forward and held Moran's hand as it came down again. In the short, silent struggle he was the stronger. Moran went down, dragging the boy with him but he wasn't able to dash him sideways against the dresser as he fell. They struggled blindly, rolling about. Eventually it was the boy who pinned the father to the floor; but as he tried holding him by the arms, on rising he received several violent blows to the head from above. Shouting out with pain he let his grip go and jumped to one side. Rose was between the two men with a heavy brush in her hands.

'I'm surprised at you, Michael,' she accused and then went to Moran's aid. 'Are you all right, Daddy? Are you all right?'

Brushing her help aside, he staggered to his feet and breathing very heavily went to sit in the chair.

'Are you all right, Daddy?' she asked again.

'I'll be all right in a minute,' he said. 'And I'm far from finished with that gentleman. If that gentleman thinks he can do anything he likes now in this house I'm telling him he'll soon have another think coming.'

It was then, coldly and deliberately, that he fixed his eyes on the shotgun where it stood beside the back door in the far corner of the room. Whether he was seriously thinking of using the gun or that he wanted Michael to think he would use it would never be known. If he just wanted Michael to think he might use it he succeeded absolutely. For the rest of that evening his son stayed close to the gun. Any time Moran moved between him and the back door he found himself tensed to spring. He would have given anything to discover if the gun was loaded but he couldn't check it. He reassured himself that Moran had always insisted that a gun should always be unloaded when approaching a house or climbing across a fence.

If it hadn't been for the heavy rain Michael would probably have left that night. In the morning he would leave and this time he would not come back. All he had to do was to get through the night. Obediently he went through the remaining gestures. Moran did not speak at all except to say the Rosary. Michael said good night to Rose but it was clear that he did not have to say good night to Moran any more. As soon as he got to his room he moved the bed so that it stood against the door and unlatched the window. He breathed a little easier when he heard his father and Rose go to bed but still he didn't sleep. Towards morning, an hour or so before Rose usually got up, he stole towards the kitchen. All the doors were ajar and he could pass through them without sound. He could hear the pounding of his heart as he reached into the corner and slowly lifted the shotgun. He took it into the hallway before opening the breach. As it made a small click he listened intently but he could hear no sound from the far bedroom. He expected to find the breach empty. The gun shook in his hands when he saw the brass of the shell. If it was loaded it went against everything Moran had preached about guns all his life; but when he took the shell from the breach he found that it was empty. Breathing much easier he put the empty shell back and returned the gun silently to its corner. In bed again he fell into a heavy sleep. Rose had to shake him awake. He dressed quickly and made a small bundle of the few clothes he wanted to take. In the living room with Rose he was careful and silent and a bit depressed. He would never repeat these small acts of morning in this room again. The youthful self-absorption was comic. He would never take the top off his boiled egg again while looking across the fields to McCabe's wall. Sentimentally, through each small act he found himself taking leave of his youth. Rose took his silence and faint air of depression as contriteness over the clash with Moran.

'Don't worry, Michael,' she said. 'All you have to say is that you're sorry when you come from school and that'll be the end of it. Your father thinks the world of you.'

'It wasn't my fault. The salt just overturned. I did nothing.'

'You know it wasn't just the salt, Michael.'

'He never lets up at me for a minute lately.'

'You know your father. He'll not change now. All you have to do is appear to give in to him and he'd do anything for you after that. He wants nothing but good for the whole house.'

'Thanks, Rose,' he smiled as he got up from the table. Her whole little speech brought him close to tears. He wanted to get out of the house before they began. Rose saw the tears and they brought tears to her own eyes. She was sure everything would be all right again. She would have a word with Moran about his early morning contriteness as soon as he got up and make certain that everything moved towards reconciliation and the unquestioning love she herself felt with her whole heart.

An early morning bread van took Michael as far as Longford, a cattle truck brought him from there to Maynooth. For a long time he had to hang around Maynooth until a priest gave him a lift into the city. It was past lunchtime and he felt weak with hunger when he walked from O'Connell Bridge to the big government offices where Sheila worked. A porter who remembered him from the last time took him up in a lift to Sheila's office.

'What are you doing here again?' she demanded sternly though she already knew.

'I'm going to England,' he said.

'When?'

'Tonight if I can.'

He told her of the fight, Rose beating him about the head with the brush and Moran sitting staring at the gun in the corner of the room. It was all too familiar to be mere invention. She telephoned Mona who would come over from her office and meet them in the canteen. He had already said he was weak with hunger. She left him with an enormous plate of chips, eggs, sausages, black pudding and tea and went back upstairs to try to telephone Maggie in London. She found her at once. Maggie would take the day off from work and meet the morning train at Euston.

'So the nest is clear at last,' Maggie said when everything was arranged. 'All the birds have flown. It's sort of sad to think of it after all the years'; but Sheila was too upset to respond. Then she rang Sean Flynn who said he would leave work and come over to meet them in the canteen. Such is the primacy of the idea of the family that everyone was able to leave work at once without incurring displeasure. In fact their superiors thought the sisters' involvement was admirable. Sheila won much sympathy and received many offers of help. 'You can make up the old work any time,' they said.

Mona was already with Michael when Sheila returned to the canteen. Soon after, Sean Flynn joined the little group. He was smiling complaisantly, glad to be part of the family drama.

'He'll be met at Euston in the morning,' Sheila announced.

'Will we all put him on the boat then?' Mona asked importantly.

'Some of us will have to anyhow,' Sheila said and then turned to Michael. 'You didn't make much of a go of it after us taking you home and everything.'

'I did my best,' he said.

'I doubt it was very much. How did we manage when we were your age?'

'The whole lot of you were there then.'

'He fell at the last hurdle,' Sean Flynn said and laughed.

Sheila met his laughter with a withering stare. He might be allowed through her into the family but it did not mean that he belonged. No outsider was allowed to laugh at anything so sacrosanct as the family.

There was not much time. The boat sailed at eight-forty. They left the table to go to the early boat train. At the harbour Sheila took charge as usual. She bought the ticket, gave him money for the journey and forced her way on board the boat where she found a purser who promised to look after Michael and to put him on the London train. By the time the boat reached Holyhead everyone he met was helpful once the story was

123

known: it was as if everybody at one time or another had run away from home themselves or had wanted to run away.

The three of them watched the boat for a long time after it left the harbour. There were tears in the girls' eyes and Sean Flynn put his arm round Sheila's shoulders as they turned away from the sea and the granite wall with the small mica glints.

'We've all gone now,' Sheila said between low sobs.

'It had to happen some time or other though maybe it could have happened in a better way,' Mona said.

'Maybe there's no good way,' a scolding note had come into Sheila's voice.

Wisely, Sean Flynn was silent.

Around the same time that the boat was sailing for Holyhead Moran was kneeling to say the Rosary.

'It doesn't look as if he'll come now,' Rose said anxiously. She had kept his dinner warm for him in the slow oven though the food was already tasteless. 'He must have gone to the girls again,' Rose continued nervously. 'He was always a great one to look for sympathy. We'll probably hear from them tomorrow. Perhaps they'll bring him back at the weekend.'

'I'm afraid he'll have to change his tune if he intends to stay here again.'

'I don't know what came over him. He told me he was sorry this morning. He was going to apologize this evening.'

'We better say the Rosary in the name of God.'

Moran took out his beads and rattled them impatiently. The light was dimming between the big trees but the stone wall along McCabe's still stood out pale and solid. Moran had to recite the Third Decade because of the boy's absence. Afterwards he sat morosely in the chair, not wishing to speak at all, just watching the light disappear. Rose turned on the lights and drew the curtains and started to make tea. Moran went to switch on the radio. Music played. He stood listening to it for a while, his hand on the knob and then, as abruptly, turned it off again. As soon as he had taken the tea and bread he stopped to loosen his boot laces.

'He's gone,' he brooded. 'They're all gone now.'

'Maybe he'll be back no later than tomorrow,' Rose tried to soothe.

'Who wants him back? Who wants any of them back? They're all gone now and who cares anyhow!'

Mona and Sheila dithered about whether to write or telegram the news home. They decided against the telegram because of its alarmist associations and wrote a short note saying that Michael had gone to London and they would be down at the weekend to tell them about the whole business. They came together on the train.

Usually Moran was on the platform to meet the train and if he was in good humour he often made little jokes as soon as he met them but this Friday night there was no sight of him even after the platform emptied. Finally they found him sitting in the car outside the station.

'We thought you hadn't come,' Mona said nervously but he didn't answer. He started the car and drove studiously out of the town.

'Michael went to London,' Sheila blurted out against the silence. 'We tried to get him to come home but this time it was no use. There was no talking to him. He'd made up his mind to go. It wasn't like the last time at all.'

'Where did he get the fare then?' Moran asked tersely.

'We gave him the fare. We had to. He threatened to go without it and he'd give Luke's name in London if he got caught.'

'He might find it wasn't that easy if he got caught.'

'Anyhow he was going to go and we felt we had to give him the fare. We rang Maggie so that he'd be met on the other side.'

'I suppose he has my name well blackened.'

'He said there was a fight. He said he was afraid of the gun.' It was Sheila's turn to attack, tired of deflecting Moran's aggression.

'I knew I'd be blackened. I'd never harm any member of the

125

family. Anything I ever did was done for what I thought was in the best interests of those concerned. Sometimes what I did might have been misguided but it was always meant for the best.' Whenever Moran turned moralistic the girls knew that some resolution had been reached.

The headlights were already lighting up the dark yew at the gate. Rose was so nervous that she did not come out to meet them at the door. They found her deep within the kitchen, pretending that she had not heard the car's return. As she quickly dried her hands and ran towards them, her excess of gladness and affection masked an anxiety that had gnawed at her since Michael first ran away.

'He went to London. They had to give him the money,' Moran announced to Rose. The two girls were able to drop their apprehensiveness for the first time since they left Dublin and they embraced Rose wholeheartedly.

'We had to give him the money,' Mona said. 'We couldn't make him come home.'

'Poor Michael,' Rose said. 'He thinks the streets of London are paved with gold and that there are girls falling out of houses everywhere.'

'He'll get his eyes opened,' Moran said.

In that one exchange the facts of his going were glossed over and instantly everyone made haste to return to the everyday. Rose made a big fry for tea as if it were a special Sunday. She kept chatting and laughing all through the meal and afterwards relayed fresh scraps of news as she washed up with the girls – new dresses and styles worn to Mass by those who had come home from England or America and how they had thought the scissors were lost and they would have to buy a new pair, but only the day before yesterday she came on them in an old boot of Daddy's; they must have fallen into the boot . . .

'There are none more blind than those who will not see,' Moran said humorously.

'Now Daddy. You know I looked day and night,' Rose protested while joining in the laughter.

'There are none more blind,' Moran repeated and laughed

even louder. They were relieved. His mood was clearing. As soon as they had the dishes dried, the room tidied, Moran suggested that they say the Rosary and they all knelt. At the very end he offered a special prayer for Michael and all absent members of the family and that no harm come to them in London. For the rest of the evening they played cards. In the silence of the card-playing, with only the sound of the trees stirring around the house outside in the darkness, Sheila more mused than asked, 'I wonder what they all are doing in London at this very minute.'

'They are probably sitting in a room just like we are,' Rose said gently to turn aside any unease the question could bring.

'Hearts were led,' Moran said vigorously. 'Let nobody fall asleep yet.'

'Don't worry, Daddy,' Mona said emotionally as she stooped to kiss him good night. 'Michael will be all right.'

'Fear not for me but for yourselves and for your children,' Moran quoted ambiguously in the same half-playful mood he had assumed all evening.

'Maggie will look after him,' Sheila chose to ignore the quotation.

'It would have been better if he'd had the manners to learn his lesson here,' Moran pronounced the words slowly, this time unmistakably in his own voice. 'Now he'll have to learn his lesson from the world. The world will not care much about him.'

'Good night, Daddy,' Sheila kissed him.

'God bless you,' Moran responded. Then both girls went to kiss Rose.

Next day was a Saturday. By the time the girls got up Rose had the fire long lit, the grey cat stretching in front of the stove.

'I thought she wasn't let in,' Mona asked as she stooped to stroke the cat. She was fond of all animals.

'She wasn't,' Rose said. 'Then Michael started to let her in. Now, sometimes, we leave her be. She feels she has rights.'

The room was warm and comfortable. They could have anything they wanted for breakfast, even grilled lamb chops, but they had orange juice, hot porridge, tea and toast. Moran came in from outside and sat by the fire and had tea. He was in marvellous good humour and started to tease them about their long sleep. They had come home expecting trouble and recrimination but found instead this pleasant warmth and good humour. They were ashamed of their fear. Their hearts were eager to respond to the warmth of the house. They would have been content with far less than what they were now being given. Mona wiped a clearing on the windowpane to look out on the dear fields and trees and the view that framed them against the far sky.

Then Mona noticed the corner of a new shed that a neighbour had built which intruded on the view. When Sheila came to the window she was outraged. 'I'm used to it now,' Rose said. 'It doesn't matter all that much.' Though Moran resented the shed he pretended to be in favour of it in order to provoke the girls more. Afterwards they walked with the old sheepdog in the fields to get a better view of the offence.

Their strong need of each other drew them together, the absence of the others. In the evening they all went into town to do some shopping. Moran sat in the car while Rose and the two girls went off together. Rose knew many people in the town and she stopped to greet them. By comparison the girls were stiff and awkward with people, unsure how to act.

'Daddy doesn't like to see me talking to too many people. He thinks it's a waste of time but the time is often wasted anyhow,' Rose confessed to them, as if she were slightly delinquent, while hurrying back to the waiting car. 'You know Daddy hates to be left waiting too long.'

The car was parked past the post office along the railings of the sunken tennis courts and he sat looking out at the people that passed by without acknowledging them or being acknowledged. He had to shake himself out of his lethargy when he saw Rose and the girls approach.

'You must have bought the town,' he said when they opened the car door.

'We hadn't the time,' Rose said. 'Or the money.'

'I'm sure you bought lots anyhow.' He hadn't grown impatient waiting. He started the car at once and drove home.

They put more wood on the fire, made tea, said the Rosary, played cards until they kissed good night, the whole world shut away outside. Moran could not have been more charming during the whole weekend. He did not need to be very charming. They had learned to accept him in all his humours: they were grateful for anything short of his worst moods, inordinately grateful for the slightest goodwill, what they barely would have accepted from an equal.

'I'm thankful for all you did for Michael,' he surprised them by saying as they waited in the car outside the railway station the next evening.

'We're sorry we couldn't get him to come home,' Mona mumbled.

'I know you did your best. That's all anybody in the family can do.'

On the platform he kissed them as the train drew in. They told him they would be down again before very long. The two sisters were silent as the train crossed the Shannon, travelling through fields. As the train was pulling into Dromod, the small platform black with people like themselves returning to Dublin at the end of the weekend, Mona said in an emotional voice, 'No matter what they say, Daddy can be wonderful.'

Sheila nodded her head in vigorous agreement, 'When Daddy's nice he's just great. He's like no other person,' and even the small white stones under the lights on the station platform took on a special glow.

Moran went out to the road and closed the iron gates under the yew after returning with the car from the station. He listened for the noise of the diesel train crossing the Plains behind the house but it had already passed. The light was beginning to fail but he did not want to go into the house. In a methodical way he set out to walk his land, field by blind field. He had not grown up on these fields but they felt to him as if he had. He had bought them with the money he had been given on leaving the army. The small pension wasn't enough to live on but with working the fields he had turned it into a living. He'd be his own man here, he had thought, and for the first time in his life he'd be away from people. Now he went from field to field, no longer kept as well as they once were, the hedges ragged, stones fallen from the walls, but he hardly needed the fields any more. It did not take much to keep Rose and himself.

It was like grasping water to think how quickly the years had passed here. They were nearly gone. It was in the nature of things and yet it brought a sense of betrayal and anger, of never having understood anything much. Instead of using the fields, he sometimes felt as if the fields had used him. Soon they would be using someone else in his place. It was unlikely to be either of his sons. He tried to imagine someone running the place after he was gone and could not. He continued walking the fields like a man trying to see.

Dark had fallen by the time he went into the house. Rose had washed up and tidied after the visit but he did not notice. She did not ask him where he had been but more than once looked at him with covert anxiety. She would feel easier if he raged or scolded. As soon as he sat at the table, she made and poured his tea. She checked that everything he needed was on the table and then asked him if his tea was sufficiently strong.

Mona and Sheila came every other week from Dublin to the house and twice a year Maggie came from London. After the long train and sea journey she would stay a day and night in Dublin with her younger sisters. The three girls had so much to tell one another that the time never seemed long enough. They all went home together on the train. They were in their flower and attracted many admirers. Moran always came alone to the station to meet them. Though he would be nervous with excitement and irritable for days before they came, he was distant and withdrawn as soon as he met them. Rose's delight in seeing them was slightly tempered by her natural watchfulness but within an hour she would have completely merged with the band of girls, joking, laughing, getting them to help with chores, always giving them her full attention and they answered to her as if she were another sister rather than their father's wife.

If Moran was in the fields she would sometimes smoke an 'outrageous' cigarette. 'I know Daddy doesn't like it but it's an occasion.'

'Smoking is no harm,' they would say in unison though they did not smoke themselves.

'Bad habits picked up in Scotland,' she would say lightly and look up as she laughed. 'Of course I smoke in front of him but he never likes it.'

'He'll not change now.'

'No, it's very unlikely he'll change.'

No matter how far in talk the sisters ventured, they kept returning, as if to a magnet, to what Daddy would like or dislike, approve of or disapprove of. His unpredictable violences they discounted simply as they might the tantrums of a difficult child. His moods were as changeable as the moods in the long day of a child and Rose could follow them now even better than they. Sometimes the moods were of pure charm, like asking one of the girls to go with him over the fields to look at the cattle as if he were inviting them to a special place in his heart.

'It's more than Rose would do nowadays – come with me to look at the cattle,' he would tease as he waited for one of the girls to dress for the fields.

'Listen to him talk now,' Rose would rail happily. 'Who did everything with the cattle when you were in bed for a whole week just before Christmas?'

'That'll do you now,' he would say indulgently.

When Moran was out of the house they often talked of Luke and Michael. Rose's inquiries went eagerly in search of Michael. He had had several jobs already – clerk, labourer, night porter in a hotel, even cook: 'Poor Michael's cooking,' Rose laughed at the vision until it hurt. 'I wouldn't like to eat in that restaurant.'

'It was a canteen but he burned someone with cooking oil and was sacked. He's on the buildings now.'

'Has he girls?'

'Girls?' Maggie said. 'He doesn't seem to mind who he has as long as they have skirts. And they go for him as if he was honey.'

'He's so young,' Rose said. 'Does he say anything about coming home at all?'

'He says he'll come home in the summer but he'll have to save.'

'Does he mind what went on?' she asked anxiously.

'Not at all. He was telling one of his girlfriends one evening about this place. She was Indian. It'd make you laugh. You'd think he was describing heaven.'

'It was all his own fault anyhow; and you know Daddy.'

'Michael isn't like Luke at all that way. He doesn't hold anything in. Once it's over it's forgotten.'

Rose didn't want to talk about Luke, or she wasn't yet ready to do so, for as soon as his name came up she changed the conversation to a shopping trip that had been proposed.

All these conversations were relayed by Rose to Moran: they were their main subject of conversation when they were alone, and she hoarded them like precious morsels. Moran had always put on such a hurt air when Luke's name came up that she assumed he didn't want to hear about him at all, that he found it too disturbing; but she learned that the opposite was true, that Moran couldn't bring himself to ask the girls. She brought to him all she knew.

Luke had qualified as an accountant but still worked with the same firm which bought old houses round Notting Hill, converted them into flats and then sold them. The firm had grown bigger. He seemed to be one of four partners. His girlfriend was English whom he had met through his work. They weren't sure if they lived together or not but they thought they did. She was tall, dark; she wasn't pretty but they supposed she could be called attractive: they didn't like her very much.

'Is she *hoi polloi*?' Rose asked humorously.

'I think her father worked in a bank,' Maggie said.

'Daddy would love it if Luke came home though he cannot say it,' Rose said.

'I told him that,' Maggie said warmly. 'I asked him, was he afraid to go home or what was wrong with him. He was rude – the way he looks at you! You never can tell *what* he is thinking.'

'What did he say?'

'He said that only women could live with Daddy.'

'He has some neck. Something's wrong with him. He won't live and let live,' Sheila added.

Maggie was more eager to talk about Mark O'Donoghue, a young man from Wexford who worked on the buildings in London. They were secretly engaged but it was a secret she told everybody, including Rose who had of course told Moran. She wanted everybody who met Mark to be as excited about him as she. Part of her annoyance with Luke was that he had been non-committal when they met in London and he had refused to say what he thought about Mark despite her tearful pressure. 'He's fine with me' was the most she could force from him by way of approval. But what she wanted most of all was Moran's approval.

Maggie brought Mark O'Donoghue home at Easter. After the boat journey they stayed the night with Mona and Sheila in Dublin. Though the two sisters had heard much about him before the first meeting they were taken aback by his appearance. He was as fair and handsome as they had been told but they were shocked by the black drainpipe trousers, the black suede shoes, the Elvis hairdo, and a dark wool jacket that was studded with little bits of metal that glittered when they caught the light.

'Good God, he's a teddy boy,' Sheila said as soon as she caught sight of him at Maggie's side on the platform.

'Daddy will have a fit,' Mona said with dismay.

When they suggested to Maggie that Mark should buy a dark suit or a tweed jacket for the important visit home she was upset and angry. What Mark was wearing was the height of fashion. It had cost a small fortune to assemble. He would not be comfortable in any other clothes nor would other clothes show him off so well; and when they saw the tears fill her eyes they did not press.

133

That evening they all went out together to a pub. Mark was charming, a good-looking man with three young women, and he drank several pints, remaining in good spirits throughout the evening. Maggie drank beer as well. Both her sisters soon saw past the good looks and glittering jacket to the kind of people he came from, the small-town poor. They felt a little sorry for him, but for Maggie's sake as well as for their own future lives together, an overwhelming desire that Moran should approve of him gradually blotted out any feelings of their own. They saw that Maggie would marry him and that their lives would intertwine with his for years to come.

On the train he drank bottle after bottle of Smithwicks at the bar. Maggie wasn't worried because he never got drunk on beer. She had tea.

'Why won't you have a beer?' he asked.

'I'd feel odd meeting Daddy after drinking beer.'

'That sounds bananas to me,' he laughed. 'But please yourself. Anyhow tea is cheaper.'

Once the train passed Mullingar she found herself getting nervous. After Longford she went and spent a long time in one of the toilets. When she returned to the bar Mark noticed that while she had combed her hair and made up her face she had also taken off her engagement ring. There was a sharp edge to his voice when he asked her where it was.

'It's in my handbag.'

'Why?'

'We didn't tell Daddy we are engaged. If I wore the ring it'd look as if we got engaged without his leave.'

'That's what happened.'

'It wouldn't look right.'

'What if the old boy can't stand me?'

'It won't matter, love. You know I love you. I know he'll like you. They all do. You look just great. Trust me. We'll do it this way.'

'Whatever you think,' he said shrugging his shoulders. As their station was the next one they took their luggage out and stood in the corridor. 'We're passing the house now.' She pointed out tall trees in the distance across fields of stone walls. Despite the beer, he had caught some of her excitement and he remained silent, stroking her hair lightly with his hand.

From deep within the shadows Moran watched them get off the train. In this quiet place where dress was conservative, all violence hidden, Mark appeared like a figure out of pantomime. Moran smiled grimly, feeling that he had the advantage, and came firmly out of the shadows. Maggie kissed him nervously and introduced the two men.

'You're welcome,' Moran said without warmth as he shook his hand.

'Nice to meet you, Michael,' Mark said. *Michael* was the form of address Mark and Maggie had agreed on since he would not call him *Daddy*. It was the kind of 'with it' thing they felt went with Mark's good looks. Moran disliked the familiarity and drove home in silence. Maggie kept up a nervous commentary on how Luke and Michael were doing in London. Moran appeared not to be listening.

'They are very economical – these cars,' Mark said after a long silence.

'They go,' Moran responded without taking his eyes from the road.

In the house it was easier, Rose making him welcome, putting hot food on the table, inviting him to eat his fill after the long journey. He smiled his sunny handsome smile but, though Rose acknowledged it brightly, he did not feel it worked and he noticed the furtive watchfulness behind Rose's charm. Everybody was watchful here. It was like moving about in a war area. What had first impressed him about Maggie was her air of separateness and superiority when they had met one Saturday night in the Legion after he had come half-pissed from the Crown. In this house it disappeared as if it had never existed. She who had never appeared to him less than confident was nervous here, cautious, careful in every word and movement.

Suddenly he was angry. 'You have a fine house here, Michael,' he said with manly aggression.

Moran looked at him but Mark did not flinch, waiting openly

for a fair answer to his salute. Moran pushed his plate and cup away from the edge of the table.

'Thank you,' he said, and the two women smiled and were able to move again. 'The family was brought up here. I suppose everything wasn't done completely right but we did all we could according to our lights. Nobody starved. We asked nobody for anything.' Suddenly he changed. 'I suppose now in the name of God that we had the tea we might as well say the Rosary and get it done early.'

He took the purse with his beads from his pocket and without waiting for any response let them spill out into his palm. He put a newspaper down on the cement and knelt where he had sat upright at the table. He waited for the others to kneel. Maggie handed Mark a newspaper and motioned him to kneel at table or chair. He raised his eyebrows but he too knelt.

'I'm afraid I have no beads,' he said looking around to Maggie's trepidation.

'You have fingers,' Moran said, and began, 'Thou, O Lord, wilt open my lips,' which never had rung out more domineeringly. Maggie recited the Third Mystery. There was a long pause when she finished. Not until she called sharply *Mark* did he realize they were waiting for him to recite the Fourth Mystery. He stumbled over the first lines, with Maggie suffering tortures in case he would be seen to be so unused to prayer as to have forgotten the words; but by the time he got to the Hail Marys he was able to fall back on the repetitive rhythms and Maggie was able to breathe easily again. He remembered to count on his fingers. As a child he had never counted on anything else. In their house prayers were never said aloud. Each child would say his own private prayers until they were forgotten about in their growing up. His mother went to church most evenings but he always thought that it was more in search of peace after the turmoil of the day than for any need to pray – the way his father went to O'Connell's bar on the corner when he was flush. Moran himself recited the Fifth Decade but still the prayers continued: Hail Holy Queen, the Litany, Blessed Oliver Plunkett, St Jude, the Grace of a Happy Death, Absent

136

Members of the Family. Mark found that as long as he made a show of mouthing the responses he did not have to pay much attention, that he could imagine who was in the Three Black-birds at this particular moment and what they were drinking. Murphy's crowd would still be throwing darts in the public bar, the single bottles of light beside the pint glasses on the counter. It came as a surprise to hear the chairs move as Maggie and Rose got to their feet. Moran dropped his beads slowly back into the black purse, still kneeling, and then lifted himself off his knees.

'They say the family that prays together stays together,' Moran said. 'I think that families can stay together even though they're scattered, if there's a will to do so. The will is the important thing.'

Then Moran began to question Mark with heavy authority: what subjects had interested him at school, what did he do before he went to England, what was he doing now in England.

'The buildings is the readiest money once you get to England,' Mark said.

'But not as you get older,' Moran said.

'I'm learning to drive.'

'Drive what?'

'A digger and a dumper. The best paid of all is if you can get to drive the crane.'

'How do you go about learning that?'

'You get them to show you after the job stops, the fellows that drive, that is.'

'How do you go about that?'

'They have to sort of like you and you buy them pints. If you buy them enough pints it goes a long way.'

'I believe my eldest son works in somewhat the same line of business,' Moran changed awkwardly.

'No. He's in renovation,' Mark explained patiently. 'They buy up old houses and convert them into flats. I've always worked on big open sites.'

'I wouldn't know,' Moran said testily. 'He doesn't choose to tell me what he does.'

'He's away with it. He's a director of that company.'

'I wouldn't know,' Moran had now had enough. 'And it wouldn't make any difference if I did. I look on all my children as equal no matter what their station in life is. Anybody they choose to bring into the family I also look on in the same way.'

Rose started to make the tea they had each night before going to bed. Mark saw that there was still a good hour to go before the pubs closed. After the tension of the long evening, the interrogation by the fire, he felt in terrible need.

'I'd like to go for a drink,' he said to Maggie.

'The nearest tavern is four miles,' Moran said drily.

'I'm sure there are some cordials in the house since Christmas,' Rose offered.

'I'd like to go out for a drink. Couldn't we borrow the car?'

Maggie stood frozen before the confrontation. So great was Mark's need to get out for a drink that it enabled him to confront Moran's formidable authority within the house.

As slowly as it seemed possible Moran took the car keys from his pocket and threw them on the table with a contemptuous little flick.

'I don't like the idea of people driving who drink,' Moran said.

'We'll be careful. We'll only have one drink or two at the most. It's just to get out of the house.'

'I can't imagine what you'd do after a week in the house if you're that wild to get out now,' Moran said sarcastically but Mark didn't hear. He had the car keys. He was already walking into the door of a strange bar, smelling the freshness of the porter, savouring the white collar.

Maggie put on her coat and went up to Moran to kiss him good night. He allowed her to kiss him but he did not return it.

So uncomfortable was the silence that Mark asked, now that he had the keys in his hand, 'Are you sure you and Rose wouldn't come with us, Michael?'

The proposition sounded so ludicrous to Moran that the very idea seemed an echo of the glittering jacket, and he began to laugh harshly. 'No, Mark. We wouldn't like to go with you but enjoy yourselves.'

It took some time for them to start the car. As they heard it drive away Moran said reflectively to Rose, 'We are made up at last. We'll have the town poor in the family next.'

'I wouldn't mind the jacket. That's just the fashion. It'll change,' Rose said tentatively.

'It's not the jacket. It's the man. There were some of those types in our battalion for a while. They could put on a show and swagger but when it came to any crunch they had no backbone.'

'He's nice-looking and he seems to suit Maggie. He looks kind.'

'I was never much on the lookout for kindness, but don't worry, Rose. If he suits her he'll suit me,' he said.

They went to bed but did not sleep until after the car was returned to the shed. A door banged and Mark's voice was loud as they came in. Then they heard Maggie's low urgings that he keep his voice down.

'That's going to be their life,' Moran said. 'Gather money, then a spree; gather more money, then another spree. It's not going to be easy to keep it going. I'll help any of my family in any way I can but I draw the line at helping to keep the sprees going.'

The following days went more easily. Maggie had always been by far the most gregarious of the girls. She was known in every house around. Now she could show Mark off. In such a quiet place the young couple was excitement and brought news. When Mark's good looks were admired Maggie blossomed and grew prettier in the praise. Usually he was given a large glass of whiskey with the customary tea and sweet cake or biscuits. He glowed in the attention and alcohol and came home to Rose's meals in high good humour. In spite of the severity of the family he was beginning to feel that it was flattering to be connected to such a house, this house that was at the centre of Maggie's being. In such a mood, at Maggie's prompting, he would search Moran out in the fields to chat. Moran saw him as no threat and was unusually indulgent. Maggie's pleasure was so intense that she could not speak when she saw the two men come together into the house. It was in the evenings, until the Rosary was said, that Moran's brooding silence, broken by occasional sallies, always had to be watched and it was the Rosary itself that Mark found hardest; but then he could take the car to the pub. He found a bar of his own in town where he had ingratiated himself with the owner and a few regulars.

A few hours before they were due to leave for the train Maggie alone, in great trepidation, went into the fields to look for Moran. She found him stretching barbed wire that had loosened on a boundary fence and he was stapling it to fresh posts. As soon as he saw her he knew at once why she had come, and waited.

'We're going today, Daddy.'

'I know. I'll drive you to the station but it's not time yet.'

'I want to know what you think of Mark, Daddy.'

'Why do you ask?'

'We are thinking of getting married.'

He let go of the strand of wire and faced her directly. 'If he does you, Maggie, he'll do me.'

'You have nothing against Mark then?' What he said had been a great deal less than she had hoped for.

'I look on all my children as equal. Anybody they choose to bring into the family will get looked on in the same way. If you marry Mark, he'll be like any other member of the family, neither more nor less. There's one thing I would say to you. I'd say it to anybody. I do not think the tavern every night is the best preparation for a great marriage.'

'That's just because it is our holidays, Daddy.'

'I sincerely hope so,' Moran said firmly.

'Is it all right for me to marry Mark then?'

'If he does you, Maggie, he'll do me. I hope you'll be happy.'

There were tears in her eyes as she kissed him. In the weeks ahead this grudging approval would grow in her mind into an ecstatic welcome of Mark by the whole family.

Rose smoothed Maggie's arms down from the shoulders,

holding her young body out at arm's length in order to give it full admiration as they took their leave. 'You have a beautiful figure, Maggie. It's a wonderful thing to see a handsome couple starting out on their lives.'

Moran drove them to the station and waited with them on the platform until the train came.

'Thanks for everything, Michael,' Mark said manfully as they shook hands.

'Please God, you'll both be happy,' Moran said.

'Thanks, Daddy,' tears were slipping down Maggie's cheeks as she raised herself to kiss him goodbye.

As soon as the train was moving Mark said, 'I need a drink. I need several drinks. I feel as if I've just got out of jail.'

'You were allowed to go anywhere you wanted.' Maggie was stung by the implication. 'Daddy even gave you the car every night.'

'I'm not complaining. It's just a feeling. No matter what you did you felt it wasn't awanting.'

'That's just a way Daddy has. He liked you very much but it's hard for him to show it. He said that he was very happy that we are going to be married.'

'We'd be married anyhow whether he was happy about it or not.'

'It's far nicer though that Daddy agrees to it.' She had taken the engagement ring from her purse and slipped it back on her finger. She raised the ring to the window so that the three small rhinestones caught the rushing light. 'The ring will never leave this hand now,' she said.

'Would you like me to bring you a beer back?' Mark asked.

'I'll come with you. We can have a drink together in the bar.'

When they reached an empty corridor between two carriages they paused and held each other in a long embrace before going on to the bar.

They were married that July in London. All the house was at the wedding except Moran and Rose. Mona was bridesmaid. Luke stood in for Moran and Maggie walked up the altar on his arm. The reception was held in a large room above the Three

Blackbirds. After the meal and the toasts there was dancing to a piano. Most of the guests were in their twenties, young men bronzed from the building sites, girls from the hospitals. Moran wrote that London was too far off of a journey for him and Rose to travel to at their age and he enclosed a cheque that covered most of the cost of the reception.

'It would be too hard on Daddy to see you married in London,' Mona and Sheila joined to counter Maggie's disappointment that Moran did not come to her wedding. 'He and Rose aren't young any more.'

As if the wedding itself was a breach they were determined not to let widen, the girls beat an even more vigorous path back to the house that summer and winter than ever before. Mona or Sheila, and often both of them together, came every weekend. They took their holidays to coincide with the hay, the only time of year when there was any stress of work now, and they helped Moran and Rose save and gather it into the sheds.

Michael broke his leg in an accident on the buildings. He came home that winter for several weeks while convalescing. All the old trouble between the son and father had been forgotten about; Michael even laughed out loud once when it came up by accident. Rose loved to see Michael home. He was more her natural child than any of the girls. When alone they could be heard chattering away and each of them would cease instinctively the moment Moran entered the room. During these chats he told Rose that he was abandoning casual labouring work as soon as he returned to London. Luke told him that he would find him a place in the City that could lead to qualifying as an accountant if he passed his exams. Already he was studying books that Luke had given him to read while his leg healed. Rose passed all this information on to Moran. 'He could be qualified now if he had minded his manners when he was at school. He always had brains enough. He had to learn manners the hard way.'

As great a pall would fall on the conversation when Luke's name came up as fell on Rose and Michael's bright chatter the moment Moran entered the room. Rose told the girls that Moran was secretly grieving for Luke, and the more they discussed it among themselves the more indignant they grew. They felt that Luke's whole behaviour was unnatural and hard and unforgiving. They all had grievances enough but there was little use in holding on to them for ever.

Luke had to be challenged. Maggie volunteered to face him. She rang him at work. He readily agreed to meet her in a little pub close to Leicester Square station. Mark came with Maggie. Luke was alone when they arrived. Despite Mark's pressing him to take a pint, he would only have a half of bitter and he nursed it through the meeting. Mark was drinking pints, Maggie halves of lager. They were dressed up and looked as if they were intending to spend the whole evening in the pub.

'What's wrong with you? You don't look sick to me,' Mark said laughingly, relaxed and prepared to be charming.

'It just does nothing for me,' Luke raised his glass.

'I hope the same will never happen here. Good luck!'

'Daddy is upset you've not gone home in all these years. He's getting old now. He wants you to go home.'

'It would do no good.'

Though tall, Luke had always been slight of build and he hadn't filled out much with the years. His eyes were clear. He was taut, watchful and hidden, in direct contrast to his younger brother's sunny good looks.

'You hold too much of a grudge,' Maggie said.

'I hold no grudge. That would be stupid. But I have a good memory.'

'Your father wants you to go home,' Mark supported Maggie.

'If he wants to meet me he could have come over for your wedding and we could have taken it from there. He just wants everything on his own ground.'

'Daddy is old now.'

'Much older men come to London to go to their daughter's wedding. I have no quarrel with his age. It's his carry-on I can't take.'

'Daddy has changed.'

'I don't believe it.'

143

'It's true,' Mark urged.

'I don't think people change, their circumstances maybe, that changes them around a bit but that's not real change.'

'This is above me,' Mark said. 'I'm getting another pint.'

'It's my round, Mark.'

'You're not drinking.'

'That doesn't matter.' He got a pint for Mark. Maggie refused a drink.

'Are you going light on your own round?' Mark teased mockingly.

'I have work to do.'

'There will be work long after you,' Maggie said.

He did not answer her but his silence was unyielding.

'You probably have as much in the bank already as would do me for the rest of my life,' Mark joked, loosened with the alcohol.

Luke still did not answer. He smiled in a gesture of amiable separateness.

Mark had finished his pint and was preparing to go to the counter for another round. 'Aren't you having anything more yourself?' he asked with the unease of heavy drinkers.

'I still haven't finished this one and I have to go in a few minutes.'

'I thought we were going to make an evening of it,' Maggie said resentfully. 'We hardly ever see you now.'

'I'll ring you. Why don't you come over to my place for dinner some evening?'

'*We* have tea in the evenings,' Mark said aggressively as he came back to the table.

'You can have tea as well. I'll give you your choice.'

'And you'll go home to see Daddy?'

'No, I said I wasn't going home.'

'It's not natural.'

'I know. I didn't choose my father. He didn't choose me. If I'd known, I certainly would have refused to meet the man. No doubt he'd have done likewise with me,' Luke laughed for the first time in the meeting.

'That's not funny,' Maggie said angrily.

'It may not be natural but it's true.'

'So you're not going home?'

'No.'

'Well then. You can forget about asking us to that famous dinner in your place,' Maggie said with confrontational sarcasm.

'I'm sorry then,' Luke rose and offered them his goodbye. He lingered uncomfortably for a moment but when they made no answer he shrugged and walked out of the bar.

'You sure come from an odd family. I think your father is easier than that brother of yours. I can't see the two of them having much to say to one another,' Mark said as soon as Luke left.

'Daddy is not near as hard as that,' Maggie protested on the point of tears.

'They're welcome to one another.'

'Daddy is different. He has his ways. I never thought Luke would get so hard. I hope you don't think *I'm* odd.'

'I don't think you're a bit odd. And I'm going to enjoy this next pint. You can't enjoy a drink with someone watching you like that.'

That Luke had refused again to go to Great Meadow went through the house in days but it was not allowed to reach Moran. Together the three girls found it unacceptable. They had assumed that time and distance would smooth all but the most angular of differences and they now feared that too much time had already passed. Beneath all differences was the belief that the whole house was essentially one. Together they were one world and could take on the world. Deprived of this sense they were nothing, scattered, individual things. They would put up with anything in order to have this sense of belonging. They would never let it go. No one could be allowed to walk out easily.

'Are you sure you put it to him right?' Sheila demanded. 'He seemed sensible enough at your wedding.'

'Mark was with me. Ask him if you want to. Oh, Luke can be very charming – excuse me – when he's not asked to do what he doesn't want.'

'Aren't we all?' Sheila responded. In the frustration the sarcasm showed clearly.

'There's no need to tell Daddy. He'd just get upset,' Rose said when she was told.

As a last resort the girls decided to send Michael to speak to Luke. They arranged to meet. Luke offered lunch and picked an Italian place near to where Michael worked. The luxury of the restaurant was a treat for Michael and he was excited and laughing. He shared his sisters' sense of family: to have lunch with his brother in such a place was important.

Luke asked about his work, his exams, if there was any help he wanted. All was well, Michael answered; nothing could be done until he qualified. They enjoyed the food, the luxury, the wine, the sense of privilege where all gathered in a fleeting act of restoration; and they had nothing to deal or sell.

'Was it all right?' Luke asked at the end of the meal.

'You could get used to it,' Michael laughed. 'It would be very easy. I have to state though that I'm here on a mission.'

'What mission?'

Michael raised his hand in mock defence. 'The sisters sent me. I'm supposed to ask you to go home to Great Meadow.'

'For what?'

'Because Daddy wants to see you.'

'Well, I don't want to see Daddy.'

'I've said my bit. I'm not saying another word.'

'The man is mad. Or that's how I remember him.'

Michael found this so funny that his sudden shout of laughter attracted the attention of nearby tables.

'I'm serious,' Luke said. 'There are lunatics, right? There are fathers who must have lunatic sons. There must be sons who have lunatic fathers. Either I'm crazy or he is.'

Michael found this so funny that he drew several looks.

'Take it easy,' Luke warned. 'You continue to go home. You know more about it now than I do.'

'Daddy's all right now. He's old. He can't do feck-all any more. You don't have to heed him. Only for Rose I don't know how he'd manage.'

'I see no reason to go back there. I found it hard enough to get out of the damned place.'

'Then don't go. I'll just tell them you won't.'

'They'll love that.'

'So what?' Michael asked.

'So what!' Luke repeated and called for the bill and paid.

Outside on the pavement, the busy street teaming around them, Michael said, 'I suppose I'm sort of fond of the old bastard in spite of everything.'

'I'm not. That's the trouble.'

'He can be all right,' Michael said as they separated. In the frail way that people assemble themselves he, like the girls, looked to Great Meadow for recognition, for a mark of his continuing existence.

When Michael brought word from the meeting Maggie was suspicious that it would be the same message she and Mark had received.

'He was nice about it. He bought me a slap-up lunch but he doesn't want to go home.'

'I suppose he just turned you round to his way of thinking.'

'No. I told him I was fond of Daddy in spite of everything. He thinks Daddy's a lunatic. He put it so cool and precise, it nearly killed me.' Freed from the constraint of the restaurant, he roared with laughter.

'I don't know which of the two of you is the worse,' Maggie said, which only increased Michael's laughter.

Maggie had her first child, a son, that summer and she and Mark took him to Great Meadow a month later. To Maggie's intense disappointment Moran evinced little interest in his grandson. Only with great pressing did he agree to be photographed with the baby in the front garden.

'Who wants to look at an old thing like me?' he complained and there was no teasing in the complaint.

'That baby is too young for travelling,' Moran said to Rose.

147

'They'd be better to hold on to their money and stay in their own house.'

'You know young mothers. They imagine the sun shines down on their child.'

'Shines out of their mouths and arses,' Moran answered sourly, and during the visit he was more drawn to Mark than to the woman and child. Mark was flattered by the attention and liked to engage Moran in man-to-man conversation. Inevitably it came round to Moran's sons.

'Michael is young and just thinks of girls but he'll settle down. There's far more nature in him than in Luke,' Mark said, though he disliked Michael. 'Luke is different. You'd never know what he is thinking. He's turning himself into a sort of Englishman.'

'Does he ever talk of coming home? You'd think he'd mention something like that after all these years.'

'We put it to him, me and Maggie, that he should go home, but he said he wouldn't.'

'Did he give any reason?'

'He said he had no interest in family matters, if you can believe that.'

'Does he see people much?'

'Mostly English. People he works with. He's always busy. I told you, Michael, he has made himself into a kind of Englishman. He sees an English girl. I don't know whether she's girlfriend or wife or mistress or what. They seem to be living together.'

'I'm sure I don't want to know about it, Mark. There are people who say we have had other existences than our present life. If that is so I must have committed some great crime in that other existence. That is all I can put Luke down to.'

As they were waiting on the station for the train to take them back to London Moran said to Maggie while Mark was getting cigarettes for the journey, 'I've learned to appreciate Mark. He seems to take an interest in our family.'

During and after the visit Moran began to spend much of his time in bed in a lethargy of spirit rather than any illness. The hay had been saved. There was no real work in the fields. It

148

was enough for Rose to throw her eye twice a day over the cattle. If there was anything wrong she would tell Moran, and they kept only dry cattle now. They were healthy and fat, ankle-deep in aftergrass.

It was the time of year Rose waited for, the rush and anxiety of the summer over, the hardness of winter not yet in. There was a great sense of space and time about the house. She was able to prepare her flowerbeds in the front garden for the winter, leaving the door open so that she was sure of hearing Moran if he called. In the orchard she picked the last of the plums and gathered some of the apples. Mona and Sheila came from Dublin every weekend. When they had the chores done she would sit with the two girls over a coffee and a cigarette, a few floating specks of dust showing in the stream of quiet sunshine that poured through the window. A few times they chatted for so long that it annoyed Moran and he shouted at them from the room.

The weekend visits allowed Rose to visit her own house by the lake, leaving Moran in the girls' care. This was a gentle renewal. There had been years when she felt that she had abandoned her own house for Great Meadow. She did not take the car. 'I'm afraid Daddy would not be long in bed if he heard I hit something with the car!' She cycled and always she brought plums and apples and jam in the cane basket on the handlebars. 'Daddy used to think I was taking half the house with me when I went after we were first married. Now he never notices that I go with anything,' she said to the girls.

'Why do you think he doesn't?' Sheila smiled as she asked. It was so quiet that it was hardly teasing.

'I don't know. I suppose he's used to it now. Daddy is strange,' she said.

'Daddy is growing old,' Sheila said matter of factly to Mona when Rose had cycled out of hearing and Mona caught her breath as if afraid and then nodded.

He never gave any explanation as to why he took to his bed at that time. No one dared question him either. It was as if it were quite normal to stay in bed without illness for part of a

149

late summer and normal again to rise and go about the house and fields as if he had never taken to his bed.

That winter Sheila announced her engagement to Sean Flynn and after that she did not come home very often. The excuse she made was that she and Sean were househunting. As if to make up for her absences Mona came alone every single weekend. Far more independent than Maggie, Sheila became engaged without benefit of Moran's approval. Sean was easygoing, anxious to be liked and Moran saw him too as no threat. Sheila had governed the relationship from the beginning but she was quick to bridle at the offhand way Moran dealt with Sean on their last visit.

In much the same way as she had wanted to go to university, she set her heart on a white wedding in June at the little village church. This Moran could not face. He would have to lead her up the aisle in front of people he spent his life avoiding, invite some of them to the reception in the Royal Hotel and pay for them to eat and drink. This he would not endure.

'It'd be simpler if she got married in Dublin,' Rose found a way out for him. She was frightened that he would refuse point-blank to attend and this wedding couldn't be hidden away in London. 'We wouldn't have to invite everybody. There'd just be the two families. And we don't have to go to the Shelbourne or Gresham. There are many small hotels. Round Harcourt Street they'd cost even less than the Royal,' Rose explained to Moran.

'Maybe that's the way we'll have to do it then. I don't know why people have to go to all this fuss to be married. Wasn't the way we were married good enough for anybody?'

'You can forget that, Daddy. All the girls nowadays want a big day. Who can blame them? They see everybody else with style and want the same for themselves,' Rose said.

Sheila cried a little when she discovered that she would not be making vows at the same altar rail at which she had received her Confirmation and First Communion, would not be coming out of the church into the shade of those great evergreens that had guarded her childhood. But she wanted Moran at her wedding. Faced with the choice, she wanted Moran more than any particular altar rail or beloved trees. 'Anyhow I never see those trees without thinking of Guinea Flanagan.' She spoke of a boy who got his name by climbing into the trees and imitating the wild cries of the guinea fowl while her class waited for the priest to come down the avenue in dry winter evenings when they were being prepared for Confirmation.

'Maybe it is just as well not to be reminded of something as silly as that on your wedding day,' she persuaded herself but her resentment surfaced when she invited Luke to her wedding without consulting anybody.

Rose managed to get Moran to leave the farm for a few days. A relative of hers agreed to look after the stock while they were away. They stayed with a brother of Rose's in Dublin and the evening before the wedding Sheila took them out to look over the new house she and Sean had bought. It was a low, detached bungalow in a new estate of a couple of hundred bungalows exactly the same, the front gardens still raw with concrete. Already in some of the back gardens lines of nappies fluttered. Inside, the house had carpets and curtains and neat inexpensive furniture. Sheila showed off each room – stating the price of each piece of furniture – with touching pride.

'Aren't you the girl that set herself up comfortably from the very beginning?' Rose embraced her in congratulation.

'Sean is worried we spent too much,' Sheila confided.

'Don't pay a bit of attention,' Rose whispered. 'Men are all like that. Get everything you need while you have the chance.'

Moran walked through the house that looked like an empty stage waiting for their lives together to begin, plainly searching for something to say but at a loss. 'It must have all come to money,' he said at last.

'I'm afraid we'll be paying for it for the rest of our lives,' Sheila answered awkwardly.

'Well I hope you'll be happy here. If you are happy that's all that counts. You can have as much of everything that's going but if you're not happy it's all useless,' he said. He was anxious to get away.

'You see, Daddy is no sooner in any place but he wants to be out the door again,' Rose teased him about what was equally true of herself.

At the door Sheila finally told them that Luke was coming to the wedding. Rose was startled and looked to Moran at once. His face clouded over at the news and was grave.

'I'm glad you invited him,' he said. 'I wouldn't like to think that any member of my family was ever excluded from a family gathering,' but his step was far from joyous as he walked away from the house.

Luke and Maggie and Michael flew over together to the wedding. Luke was flying back to London the same evening. Both Michael and Maggie had taken a few days off and were going down to Great Meadow.

'Please don't do anything to upset Daddy,' Maggie pleaded as the plane prepared to land.

'Of course not. I won't exist today,' Luke answered.

'What do you mean by that?' she asked anxiously.

'It's Sheila's big day. To draw attention to myself would hardly be good manners.' He wore black shoes, a dark pinstripe suit and a deep red tie and he looked very sober by Michael's side, whose suit was a flashing blue. They took a taxi from the airport to the church and were the first to arrive. On the empty concrete outside the church if Luke was nervous he showed no sign of it as they waited, smiling reassurances back to each of Maggie's silent inquiries. Michael appeared to find the whole situation amusing and several times broke into unsuppressed laughter.

'I'm glad you find everything so funny,' Maggie said sharply which sent him again into peals of laughter.

'I can't take it any other way.'

'Take what?' she asked, exasperated.

'The whole set-up,' he laughed. 'The whole bloody lot of us and yer man at the helm.'

'It's one way to deal with it,' Luke said quickly to calm Maggie. 'I'm sure there are worse ways and worse set-ups.'

The groom and his family were the first to arrive. Sean Flynn introduced them quickly to Maggie and the two brothers.

'I suppose we should be all going in,' Sean said.

'I'll wait till the bride gets here,' Luke said and the three waited on. Sheila and Rose and Mona and Moran all came in the same car. Mona was the bridesmaid. After he had embraced Sheila and Mona, Luke shook hands formally with Rose and Moran.

'I'm glad you got here,' Moran said darkly.

'I'm glad to be here.'

'We better be going in,' Moran said.

'We never see you nowadays except at weddings,' Sheila said to him out of nervousness.

'Aren't they the best of all places?' he responded. 'Especially when it is your wedding, Sheila.'

'We better be going in,' Moran said again.

Sheila took his arm and they walked in silence up the aisle to where Sean Flynn and his brother waited at the altar rail. Only once during the ceremony did the happy couple's eyes meet and it was in mutual sympathy at what they had agreed to put one another through.

Photos were taken outside the church while the wind blew newspapers about on the concrete and women placed steadying hands on hats and veils. Confetti was thrown. A car with white streamers took them down the road to the Avonmore Hotel. A long diagonal handle crossed the curtained glass of the hotel door.

Inside, a horseshoe desk in the hallway faced the open door to the reception room where a long table was laid. The young priest who had married them sat at the head of the table and the two families faced one another across its narrow board. Sherry or whiskey was offered but most people took orange juice. Those who drank thought it was more polite to take the sherry. Except for the priest's promptings it was clear that they could have gone from the soup to the chicken to the sherry trifle without pausing for speech or toast. Moran made the longest speech, stressing the importance of the family. There were times when the sense of his own importance seemed to overwhelm him but never sufficiently to lose thread of the grave and carefully crafted speech. His old practice at writing letters stood him in good stead. By the time he sat down there were tears in Rose's and the girls' eyes. In contrast, the father of the bridegroom was the picture of acute misery as he stumbled through the whole of one short sentence welcoming Sheila into his family. While he spoke his enormous hand encircled his sherry glass as if it were a stalk of grass.

If there had been a great show of music and drinking and dancing it might have hidden the awkwardness of the occasion. Only the worn face of Sean's mother was a study of pure emotion. He had been her first boy, her beloved. From an early age she had encouraged him at school, protecting him from the rough work of the farm; at times she had even fed him separately from his brothers and sisters. During the long summers when he came home from boarding school she made sure that he was able to read or go on walks even when his sisters were pressed into farm work. He was her special one. One day she would kneel and watch him raise the Host in the local church and after she was gone he would say Mass for her soul. When he entered the civil service instead of continuing to Maynooth, the disappointment stayed with her like a physical injury for months. Now she was losing him to another woman and he was taking on the mere life of any man with a woman. Her eyes were mutely fastened to him as he was getting ready to leave. When he took her in his arms – 'Mind yourself, Mother!' – at last she broke into the relief of tears. She watched the two heads framed in the back window of the car taking them to the airport disappear in the traffic. He did not look back once.

Before Sheila left with her husband she went up to Luke. 'Now that you have found the way you'll have to come home more often.'

'I hope you'll both be very happy,' he replied and though she kissed him warmly she made it clear that she knew that he was avoiding answering her.

He was quiet throughout the afternoon, listening attentively to anybody who spoke to him, asking polite questions, smiling, raising his glass. He sat between Mona and Michael and as Moran did not look his way there was no difficulty until the meal ended and people were preparing, with relief, to go their separate ways. Moran could be seen to be more obviously avoiding Luke. He stood in a cloud of moral injury. Noticing this, Luke went directly up to Moran. Seeing their brother go straight up to their father, the girls froze in an old fear of violence.

'I want to thank you,' Luke said.

'For what?' Moran asked.

'For the meal, the day, for everything.'

'I hope it never comes to such a state that you have to thank your father for a meal.'

Luke bowed to Rose who was straining close to tears. 'I have to thank someone.'

'Aren't you travelling further than this after all these years?' Moran asked as his son seemed about to turn away.

'I have to be back in London this evening.'

'For what?'

'I have work to do there.'

'There'll be work long after you're dead and gone.'

'I know that but it will not be my work,' Luke said with the first and only hint of firmness that day.

'God help you,' Moran said.

'Goodbye then. If you are ever in London it would be a pleasure to see you.'

'We'll not be in London.' Moran refused his son's hand.

As he was about to go to the airport Luke said to Maggie, 'You see, I kept my promise: I did not exist today.'

'You could have made more of an effort after all this time,' Maggie said reproachfully. She had left her son with a sister-in-law in London in order to be free to go to the wedding and to Great Meadow for a fortnight afterwards.

'It was the best I could do,' he said. 'I left Ireland a long time ago.'

'We all left Ireland,' Michael, who was standing with them, chuckled. 'I'm afraid we might all die in Ireland if we don't get out fast,' and he laughed louder still at his own elaboration. He too was going home to Great Meadow that evening.

The small car was full as it headed out of the city, Mona, Maggie and Michael crammed in the back. Moran drove in silence. Rose, sitting next to him, tried to lighten the slow journey with delicate titbits of small talk, each ploy more of an open suggestion to the others rather than any statement or judgement of her own. 'So we've lost Sheila,' she said at last.

'You thought you'd got rid of me but you still have *me* to put up with – large as life,' Maggie responded.

'We did our best but weren't able,' Michael said.

'You are hardly the man to speak,' Rose reminded him.

'I was only joking.'

'No one is ever lost to the family unless they want to be,' Moran said stolidly as if reciting a refrain.

'I wonder how poor Sheila will get on with her new in-laws,' Rose said. 'You know how particular she is about people.'

'They appeared to be decent hardworking people,' Moran said.

'The mother of the groom didn't seem to be enjoying herself very much,' Maggie said.

'The poor woman did look upset. I suppose it was very strange to her.'

'Or Sheila was stealing her darling boy.'

'I suppose it is the old story,' Moran said but he did not say what the story was. They were relieved that he had been drawn out of his silence.

By the time the car got to Longford they were tired and cramped. Moran did not offer to stop. 'If we say the Rosary now we'll have that much out of the way by the time we get home.'

'That makes good sense,' Rose added.

'We offer this Holy Rosary for Sheila's happiness,' Moran began.

The murmur of 'Glory Be to the Father' following 'Hail Mary' and 'Hail Mary' and 'Our Father' was as smooth and even as the purr of the engine passing Dromod, Drumsna and Jamestown. Once Michael tried to nudge Maggie into irreverent laughter as she recited her Decade but the elbow she gave him in return was sharp enough to alter his merriment. The last prayer ended as they came to the bridge in Carrick. No one spoke much afterwards except to murmur the names of the houses they passed.

'We're home!' Michael said as soon as the dark yew above the gate came into sight.

'I'm dying for a cup of tea,' Rose said and everyone in the car strained at the weariness and the relief of being able to stretch limbs and breathe in the open air and walk about.

Sheila and Sean spent the week of their honeymoon in Majorca and then came straight to Great Meadow to be with the others during the last week of their holidays. Not for years had the house been so full. Michael was moved to a storeroom at the back to make way for the couple. He was seldom in the house, always out late at dances or with girls, often sleeping well into the early afternoon. Moran and he got on well enough now, by ignoring one another mostly.

Moran was more focused on his new son-in-law. He asked him about his job, his ideas, his ambitions. Sean expected to be liked without effort. He answered Moran lazily, smiling with tolerant indulgence at his questioner. This irritated Moran intensely, and the cost of the wedding reception the week before was fresh in his mind. The attack came without warning.

'What do you mean *you* don't think much of the civil service?'

'It's a job. That's all. You can't say much more for it. It's no big deal.'

'You must be joking,' Moran said derisively.

'It's not everything. There must be more to life than that.'

'You mean a good dry job stretching to infinity with a pension at its end is of no importance? You must be talking of another world.'

'I still think it is far from everything,' Flynn defended as well as he was able.

'I see you have a lot of growing up to do. You can think those things when you are single. You are a married man now.

157

I expect more maturity than that from the members of my family.'

'There's more to life than security. There are even people who think it is the death of life,' Sean tried still to defend his ground but Moran was content to retreat into silence.

Sheila was furious when she learned of the attack. 'I was never so insulted all the times I was in his house. Luke was right when he said years ago that he has the manners of a dog,' she said emotionally to Rose.

'Daddy didn't mean anything,' Rose said.

'Didn't mean anything?' she repeated with angry sarcasm. 'You must be joking.'

It was far from easy for her when she had to face Moran directly. 'I see you are taking to cutting down your visitors to size nowadays as well.'

'I said nothing to your husband other than to put him right about a few bald facts of life.'

'You seem to forget he's a visitor in your own house.'

'He's a member of the family now like everybody else.'

'He is if he chooses to be,' Sheila said hotly. 'He's not here to be insulted.'

He did not respect Sean. Now he despised him for running to a woman with his story. He was furious at his daughter's defiance of his authority. 'I'll be hard up when I have to ask you what is good or bad manners in my own house.'

'You might learn a few decencies if you did.'

'I have meadows to cut,' he ground out. 'Go and trim that poor husband of yours if you want something to trim. I'd say you're the man for the job all right.' Before she had a chance to answer he had gone into the fields.

The forecasts promised several days of hot weather and because he had help in the house Moran decided to cut all the meadows. For hours they heard the clatter of the mowing arm circling the fields, the roar of the tractor closing and moving away. When Moran did not come in for his tea Rose and Maggie brought a can of sweetened tea and sandwiches out into the fields. They walked over the swards of two cut meadows. Only a thin strip was still standing in the centre of the third meadow and they waited on the headland, watching the grass shiver and fall in front of the arm. Two young hares bounded free as the grass narrowed into the last sward. 'They just got out in the nick of time,' Rose said with relief. 'Daddy hates to kill them but they can't be seen in the grass.' The young hares paused in bewilderment for a moment after they had run clear but then, seeing the roaring tractor turning once again, they bounded from the field and were gone. Moran noticed the waiting women as he circled and as soon as he cut the last sward he stopped the engine. The cut field looked completely empty and clean. As Rose and the girls were crossing the swards to the tractor they almost stumbled over a hen pheasant sitting on her nest. They were startled that she didn't fly until they saw feathers on the swards. The legs had been cut from under her while she sat. Her eyes were shining and alive, a taut stillness over the neck and body, petrified in her instinct.

'The poor thing,' Rose said. 'Still sitting there.' Neither could bring themselves to look again.

'You got a hen,' Rose said as she handed him a mug of tea, laying out the sandwiches on the red hood of the tractor.

'I know. You can't see them in the grass. Anyhow the hares escaped.'

'Where's the married couple?' he asked as he finished eating.

'They went for a walk.'

'They'll not need walks in the next few days. They'll have their fill of exercise. There's just the last meadow to knock. We'll either win all or lose everything this week.'

As they gathered what was left of the sandwiches and tea, preparing to leave the meadow, the tractor spluttered but would not start. Moran had to get down from the tractor. He fiddled about with some wires and the fuel pump as Rose and Maggie waited by anxiously. It spluttered when he tried the starter a second time and then caught. 'I think the only person that knows more than Daddy about that tractor is Henry Ford,' Rose said as they left the meadow. It must have been a statement of pure feeling for Moran was not mechanically minded and the tractor was an old Porsche.

He let the swards lie there till the evening of the next day when he shook them out with the tedder. When he was younger he would have cut field by cautious field but now that there was help in the house he was prepared to risk them in one throw rather than to face the long drudgery alone with Rose.

All that was left of the hen was a little scattering of down and feathers on the drying swards. 'A fox or a cat or a grey crow – who knows . . . ?'

The next morning a white mist obscured the dark green shapes of the beech trees along the head of the meadows and their sandals made green splashes through the cobwebbed pastures. A white gossamer hung over the plum and apple trees in the orchard. A hot dry day was certain. Not even by evening would there be a threat of rain. No work could be done until the sun burned the mists away and dried the swards. Rose cooked a huge fry served with brown soda bread and a pot of steaming tea. They would not have another leisurely meal till night and by then they would be too tired to eat. Moran was happy at breakfast, enjoying the certainty of good weather, the house full of help and that his gamble with the weather looked like coming through. By evening most of the hay would be saved and it could be put out of mind for another year.

'Did they make much hay in your part, Sean?' he asked pleasantly as he picked carefully at the black pudding and sausage.

'Hay and some silage when the summers were bad.'

'You must be well used to it then?'

'Not really. The others worked at the hay. I had to study in the summers.'

'Study couldn't have been much use to you in the summer,' Moran said carelessly.

'Great use. Texts could be read for the year ahead. It gave a great head start once classes began,' he answered readily and it caused an uncomfortable silence. All the Morans had to help

160

work the land since they were small. There had been clashes over the rival demands of school and harvesting, planting or cutting turf.

'In my opinion there is too much made of studying,' Moran said. 'You either have what it takes or you don't.'

'You won't get very far in any studying without work.' Sean's refusal to yield the point only sharpened hostility.

'You can say that again,' Sheila said supportively.

'You take the high road and I'll take the low road and I'll be in Scotland before you,' Moran whistled as he rose.

He went out into the meadows. The swards weren't dry yet so he made several small adjustments to the tedder. The clash with Sean hadn't improved his humour: he was anxious. Most years he never got through haymaking without breaking machinery and today he would be rowing in front of the whole house. He began to row the flat parts of the meadows first and as soon as Rose heard the tractor working she gathered all the others and led them out, making little jokes and sallies which betrayed her own anxiety as they went through the orchard.

The tedder was sweeping the hay into thick wheaten rows, leaving the ground between the rows as swept as a lawn. Moran sat stiffly on the tractor, all the time anxiously looking behind him at the pins as they turned, sweeping to left and to right.

'You'd think the tractor and Daddy were parts of one another,' Rose said.

They started at once to pitch the rows into haycocks. Rose was skilful, as was Michael when he wanted to work, and today he wanted to show off his speed and strength. He pitched and gathered in the heavy hay. The dry grass made delicious rustles against the forks. Rose trimmed the haycocks while he moved ahead and soon they were springing up in lines where the rows had been. All the girls worked well except Sheila who was more concentrated on Sean than the work. Though he was trying with his whole heart he didn't know how to use the tools and was more in the way of the others than any help. 'A drink of water in the meadow would be of more use,' Moran said to himself as he watched the useless flailing movements. 'He'll hurt somebody yet.'

Then old Ryan, a retired schoolmaster, came out from his house far back above the meadows edged by trees and he leaned on the wall to watch them work.

'I don't mind at all of course but that woman of mine is beginning to complain,' Michael mimicked Ryan and a low ripple of laughter ran through the girls but Sheila watched him, hawk-eyed at first, thinking he was making fun of Sean. So pleased was Michael with the response that he guffawed as he pitched the next forkful which increased the merriment. When Moran had rowed all the flat ground he stopped the tractor and came over. They all stopped for a drink, a mixture of milk and water in the can.

'You are getting on like a house on fire,' Moran said almost gratefully. 'The easy bit is done,' his voice sounded anxious. 'I never seem to get out of that high ground without some misfortune.'

'If you can't do it, Daddy, nobody can,' Rose said but her encouragement only earned a testy look.

'You see old Ryan out on the wall gaping already,' Moran said. 'I'm sure he'd love to see something smash. That's all this country seems to be able to do – *gape*.'

'I don't mind at all but the woman has started to complain,' Michael mimicked again but Moran did not laugh. He looked at his son coldly and turned back to the tractor.

Twice he went safely round the high ground but close to a beech tree they heard the harsh clang of the pins striking a root or a rock. The tractor stopped. Moran climbed down to inspect the tedder. They all stuck their forks in the ground and moved towards the beech tree.

'It's the damned beech roots again,' Moran said as he examined the twisted pins.

'How many are broke?' Mona asked.

'Only two. I just got it out of gear in time.'

'You could change the pins,' Michael suggested.

'You can't change the ground.'

In a way it was a relief to him that the pins had finally broken. He had no confidence that he could row the hay on the uneven ground. Now at least his dread was at an end.

Rose watched carefully. 'If Daddy can't get it to work nobody can.'

He looked at her angrily, as if the statement itself was deeply compromising; yet it was one he could not reject. 'We'll just have to go back to the old rake and fork. Thank God there's no appearance of rain. If we hang round this tractor much longer curiosity will bring Ryan across that bloody wall.'

They were coming close to the end of the rows when old Mr Rodden and his sheepdog appeared in the field. He entered unobtrusively under the barbed wire between the trees in the outer corner. He wore a straw hat and flannels and wide red braces over the neat white shirt. The collar was closed. He wore a tie and tiepin in spite of all the heat. Both Rose and Moran went towards him at once with smiles and outstretched hands. Moran considered it an honour to have him in the meadow. Rodden was a Protestant. His farm adjoined Moran's but it was at least six or seven times larger and he had lately handed it over to his son. Though Moran had been a guerrilla fighter from the time he was little more than a boy he had always insisted that the quarrel had never been with Protestants. Now he identified much more with this beleaguered class than his Catholic neighbours. No matter how favourably the tides turned for him he would always contrive to be in permanent opposition.

'I came', Rodden said, 'to congratulate the newly married couple. I heard they were home. And because the machine was idle.' He wished Sheila and Sean many years of happiness and brought a message from his wife inviting them to tea at four before they went. He praised the work and weather and then asked, 'Why aren't you using the tedder? It'd save hours.'

'I just broke the pins. I never seem to be able to work it on that high ground.'

'Have you no spare pins?'

'Lots.'

He made Moran replace the broken tines while he made several small adjustments. Then he instructed Moran to spin the tines slowly and after watching them a bit made further adjustments before he was finally satisfied that they were level. 'I think it will work on any ground now,' Rodden said. Moran then deliberately started to row the roughest ground while Rodden leaned on his stick watching. To Moran's disbelief the tedder worked the rough ground as if it were a table. After watching for a while Rodden waved his stick to signal that he was about to leave. Moran stopped the tractor and walked Rodden in the manner of local courtesy to the point where he wanted to leave the meadow. The girls and Rose and Sean waved while Michael caught the beautiful black and white collie for a parting pet.

'It never tedded that ground so well. How did you manage to do it?' Moran inquired as he left him at the fence.

'It was nothing. It was just that bit tight.' Rodden had been taught as a child that any boasting was a symptom of inferiority. 'I only made a few small adjustments.'

Rose and Sheila brought a can of hot tea from the house and sandwiches they had cut early in the morning, ham and salad and chicken. They all sat round a half-made haycock and dipped their mugs in the can, taking the sandwiches from their cardboard box. Everybody was already too tired to talk much or even eat heartily. The sun was uncomfortably hot. Nobody spoke about Rodden or the tedder.

When Moran went back on the tractor he drove it very fast between and around the beech trees. It was as if he was determined to put Rodden's adjustments to the test, but they held. No matter how he drove the tines kept sweeping the hay cleanly and sweetly into rows.

'Henry Ford seems to be going great guns now,' Michael teased Rose when they were pitching close to one another. She looked at him reproachfully and turned away. None of the girls said anything.

In an hour Moran had all the fields rowed. Hours of hard dreary raking in by hand had been saved. After he climbed from the tractor to join the others gathering the rows he spent some time examining the adjustments Rodden had made. They told him little. In his heart he knew that he would never find that setting again except by luck. As soon as he took his place with the others gathering and pitching in the rows he saw that Sheila and Sean were missing. 'Where is the pair gone?' Moran asked sharply.

'They've gone to the house,' he was told evasively.

'What for?'

'They didn't say. They just went.'

After only an hour Sean's hands were blistered and raw. The girls' hands were blistered too but they knew how to handle the tools. When Sean rose from the midday tea and sandwiches he was so stiff he could hardly move. He told Sheila – of all the girls she had most resented this work as a child – and she led him to a separate row where they could gather at their own speed. Alone they were happy. They were so absorbed in one another that they seemed to be unaware of the others pitching and gathering furiously in rows only a few yards away. They exchanged whispers, laughing as they leaned their foreheads together and then Sean tipped Sheila slyly sideways into the little pile of hay they had gathered. She rose blushing and flustered, still hardly aware of the others, and soon they were laughing together as before. As a defence against the couple the others tried to shut them out by driving themselves harder but already they were flagging in the still heat of the midday. Sheila and her husband were crossing the fence on the edge of the field before they were noticed leaving. They walked hand in hand. When they thought the copper beech hid them from the meadows Sean drew Sheila towards him by the shoulder and kissed her long on the mouth. Everyone in the field except Moran saw them kiss by the copper beech and then go arm in arm towards the house. No one spoke in the intense uneasiness, but they were forced to follow them in their minds into the house, how they must be shedding clothes, going naked towards one another . . . , as the forks sent a rustle through the drying hay. They hated that they had to follow it this way.

It was more disturbingly present than if it were taking place in the meadow before their very eyes. It was even there when they tried to shut it out. 'You'd think they could have waited,' Michael said quietly, in agreement with the resentment he felt all about him. It was as if the couple were together disregarding the inviolability of the house, its true virginity, with a selfish absorption.

'Mark has friends in London, the Creegans. We were at their wedding,' Maggie said. 'Once when Mark was away I went to visit them and missed the last train. They had one room and a large bed. I wanted to sleep on the floor but Rita wouldn't hear of it. She insisted I sleep next to her on the outside of the bed, Creggie in at the wall. After a long time I heard Creggie say, "Is she asleep?" and Rita, "Can't you wait?" I was afraid to breathe. The shaking was awful. Someone's leg touched me and I had to stuff the bedclothes in my mouth. I nearly died.'

'Poor Maggie,' Rose said with humour as well as sympathy. 'The things you have to put up with once you leave home.'

As soon as Moran stopped the tractor the haymakers split into separate groups. Rose and Moran worked together. Mona and Maggie gathered in for Michael to build a separate row. They built at much the same pace. Michael was now stronger in the meadow than Moran. The haycocks started to spring up faster in the rows than at any time since morning.

'That pair must intend spending the rest of the day in the house,' Moran said irritably after a long while.

'Sean's hands were all blistered. I'm afraid the meadow was a bit of a shock,' Rose tried to make light of their absence.

'He wasn't much use though the poor fellow tried his best. He was brought up to be the priesteen.'

When the couple did come back to the meadow they were washed and combed and dressed in new clothes. Sheila brought a can of sweetened tea. Everyone drank from the can and avoided looking at them or meeting their eyes except for Moran.

'Sean's hands are blistered from the forks. We're going over to Mrs Rodden for tea.' Sheila's voice quavered as she explained.

'Mrs Rodden will have many a story to tell,' Rose was the only one to speak to them as they left.

Sheila was defiant and determined not to be bullied. In a simple way she was already staking out her position within the family. She would belong to the family but not on any terms. She knew instinctively that she could not live without it: she would need it, she would use it, but she would not be used by it except in the way she wanted.

'Were you told about the moonlight bathing parties at Kilronan when she was young?' Rose asked when they came back from the tea.

'We were,' Sheila said. 'And how they did everything then that the smart ones think they are doing now for the first time.'

It had grown cooler in the meadow. The couple tried to help but they were not wanted. Everybody was too tired to talk. So that they did not feel ostracized Rose asked them to help bring more tea and sandwiches from the house.

The shadows of the beech trees lengthened across the rows and they worked on without knowing what they were doing, pitching and sweeping mechanically. Sometimes they would be so tired that they would find themselves just standing in the field, staring up the rows in a trance. It was relief and peace when the light began to fail and when they found their clothes becoming damp they stopped. The sky looked safe. When they were fresh again in the morning they would get what was left up in a few hours; then they would have an easy day heading and tying down the cocks. Moran and Michael were the last to leave the meadow.

'God bless you, son. That was a great day.'

Out on the road passing cars had their headlamps on. Across the road, somewhere in the demesne, a single pigeon was still cooing its hoarse throaty call as they dragged their feet through the orchard to the lighted house.

In the morning they all ached but there was no rush of work. Around noon, slowly and leisurely, they put what was left of the rows into cocks. The weather held. Then they raked and tidied, combing and heading the haycocks already up, tying

167

them down with binder twine. At the weekend the weather broke. As the warm rain swept across the fields and beat against the windows there was just time enough to savour the safety of the hay in the meadows, the rain slipping down the combed sides of the cocks. They did not need good weather any more. In a week or two they could be taken to the shed between showers on any windy day. Rose and Moran would have to do that alone.

As soon as the rain came the house began to scatter. A telegram came for Maggie to go back to London. Her son was not well and she left at once. During the rearing of hay it was as if she had almost forgotten that she had ever gone away from Great Meadow and married. All the others except Michael went with her to the airport. He stayed on alone for most of a week, helping Moran at odd jobs round the house during the part of the day he was out of bed and they got on well together. The evening he left, Rose said reflectively to Moran before they knelt for the Rosary, 'I suppose it'll be long before the house is ever as full again.'

Moran looked at her as if it were wrong or unlucky to say such things. The house was to be as full again only once more.

Nothing but the years changed in Great Meadow. Rain came down outside for days at a time as Rose moved carefully about within. When the soaked ground dried in hard winds and Moran moved slowly about outside she had breathing space again.

Weekends there was excitement in the house, for Mona now came home from Dublin almost every one. The most beautiful of the girls never married. She had many admirers and kept company with a number of men, bringing several of them home with her for weekends – quiet, deferential, generally older men, content to move within the authority of her beauty without making any serious demands; and if they did they were let go at once. As none of the men posed any threat to Moran he was always amiable, sometimes charming, for he seldom had new company and he seemed to enjoy the casual companionship. Though Mona's visits were the least noticed or talked about in the house, they too, in time, came to be depended on completely. She became the most reliable link with the outside world that increasingly shadowed their lives.

Maggie had a second child in London at the same time that Mark O'Donoghue lost his job and she came home to Great Meadow with the two children, planning to stay six months. Mark remained in London to look for a better job and to save for a deposit on a house. Moran did not welcome the move. While she was in the house he spent days in the fields or sheds and the atmosphere was tense when he and the young children were together inside the house. She left after two months, too proud and dependent to blame anything connected to Great Meadow for her early departure. She planned to return for the usual three weeks in summer. Back in London Maggie discovered that Mark had drunk everything he had earned while she was away and no money was saved. She put the children into day-care and went back to nursing full time. From then on she would always have her own money.

'Maggie and her children went back to London. They were welcome to stay with Rose and me under this roof as long as necessary,' Moran wrote in a letter. 'But I am very glad to see her go back to Mark. A wife's place is with her husband.'

Sheila came regularly too to the house but her visits were the most circumspect. She came with Mona on weekends with Sean or when Maggie was home from London. She had three children in three years and the perfect excuse when Moran complained she came less often than the others. Her old resentment of Moran was quick to show whenever he began to assert himself. She could not bear to hear him shout at any of her children.

'You'd think those children were brought up in a field,' he roared at her during one visit when their uninhibited playfulness got on his nerves.

'Well, they'll go back to that field,' she met him angrily, rounded up the children and left.

'There was no need to take a few shouts all that seriously,' Moran said but she never again brought her children to the house except for very brief visits. They were clever and confident. She did not want that confidence damaged in the way she felt her own had been. She knew that her loyalty was probably ambiguous, that the deepest part of herself was bound to her sisters, this man and house. That could not be changed; but she wanted no part of it for her children: doors would be open to them that had been locked to her, their lives would be different.

In a more sporadic way Michael too kept returning. Generally he arrived unannounced. Moran had given up trying to bend him to his will and was content to leave him to his own devices, glad to see him at all. Some gestures and mannerisms were clearly taken from the father but his nature was not dark. There were times he came and threw himself willingly into the work of the farm, getting through as much work in a day as Moran would in a week on his own and then he would leave as suddenly as he had come. 'He helped me on the bog. He brightened the whole week for Rose and myself. Michael was marvellous,' Moran wrote to Maggie after one sudden visit.

In much the same way as he had stopped school and left Great Meadow he married. In Dublin he had turned to his sisters, in London to his brother.

'What does she want?' Luke asked when Michael told him that he had met an English girl, a teacher, and that she was pregnant.

'She wants to marry me, of course.'

'What do you want to do?'

'I'm not sure. She's twenty-eight.'

'That doesn't matter if you're fond of her. You can live together till the child is born if you're not sure. Then you both can make up your minds what you want to do.'

'She'd never agree to that. She's English but she's Catholic. In ways they are far stricter than we are.'

'She can't be all that strict,' Luke said drily but changed when he saw his brother's discomfort. 'What do you like about this girl?'

'I never met anybody before who made me feel important,' Michael said emotionally and it was the older brother's turn to be embarrassed.

'Do you think it will be all right to get married?' Michael asked.

'Of course I do. If that is what you both want.'

'Should I ask our father anything?'

'Not unless you want to. I'd just go ahead if I were you. What's her name?'

'Ann Smith. The sisters won't like it, that's for sure,' he chuckled happily.

She was a swarthy, handsome woman, definite in her ways and clearly infatuated with Michael. Her entire English family turned out as a solid front for the wedding and that day all the Morans, in their different ways, were made to feel what they were – immigrants. Mona and Sheila came over for the wedding. All the girls took against Ann Smith. They searched for flaws but the real flaw was that they saw her as an interloper who would never be allowed within their own closed circle. She was the immigrant within the family. Michael took her straight from the wedding to Great Meadow.

Because of his youth and history and general unpredictability the news that Michael was marrying an English teacher was received with humorous incredulity.

'Poor Michael,' Rose laughed affectionately. 'I find it hard to see him shaping up as head of a house.'

'The likes of him often does the best,' Moran supported. They both took to Ann Smith and would not listen to the girls' criticisms.

'She's a good sensible age. It wouldn't do if Michael – God forgive me – got some skit like himself. She was busy doing degrees and diplomas till now. She'll be able to support them both while he gets his qualifications. When you come to think of it didn't the poor fellow fall on his feet?' Rose argued with humorous affection.

'If she suits Michael I am quite sure she suits me,' Moran stated. 'As far as I'm concerned she's just another daughter.' The girls listened in silence to what they could never accept. They had been brought up to keep the outside at an iron distance and now their father was welcoming it into the house.

Moran had grown noticeably careless about his dress, he who had always dressed with as much care for town or church as if he were stepping out to take on the world and it took all of Rose's watchful eyes to keep him presentable. They had two pensions now, the old age added to the military. Whether the hay was won or lost grew matterless. The bulk of the cattle was sold before the grass died and the few that were left managed on what they could get under hedges about the fields. A fall of snow that set their neighbours worrying about sheds and fodder became a pleasant break that helped time pass. In the still world, the white Plains glittering above them, they cut down small trees that were covered with ivy and they stood glowing from the exercise in the dry air to watch cattle tear hungrily at the dark ivy leaves. They had plenty of money now, Rose kept reminding him, and they did not need to slave at land any longer. They had more money than they needed, more money than they could spend, more money now than they had life but this did not give Moran any rest. Often in the evenings he spent hours calculating what he had, what was being spent, what losses were accumulating.

He took to writing letters again. There wasn't a week he didn't write to Maggie in London or to Michael. He still went to the post office to post letters and collect mail but Rose drove him there and waited outside in the car. Annie and Lizzie continued to run the post office and it still shone. Their aversion to dirt had now acquired the force of law and anybody with dirty boots or wellingtons no longer tried to enter but conducted their business from outside, the door opened for their orders and money to be handed in and opened again for groceries or letters or change to be handed out to them by the clean-heeled customers waiting within. The floor was incredibly worn but it had taken on the soft glowing white of endlessly scrubbed deal.

Annie and Moran observed a careful neutrality in one another's presence. By now they knew one another too well but once he left the little room he was no longer safe. Few were.

'How is Mr Moran nowadays?' a customer asked slyly as soon as he left.

'Not well. He was never well but he was always good at taking care of himself, God bless him,' Annie held her head low over the book of stamps until the ripple of appreciative laughter died. 'They say there wasn't a thing wrong with him when their place flooded last week but he hadn't time to think about himself for *two whole days*.'

The burst of laughter was so carelessly dismissive that it seemed to destroy at once an idea that Moran had tried to impose with ferocious will all his life.

In case the laughter could spread to her own authority Annie was quick to rein it in. 'Maybe he isn't all that well any more. I'm afraid he is going now like the rest of us, God help us all.'

'Do you remember when we first met at Annie's?' Rose said out of memory and affection one wet evening they were driving away from the post office.

He did not answer. She changed the gears awkwardly to slow down while crossing the narrow bridge. 'God, Oh God, woman, can't you concentrate on what you're doing? Haven't I told you day in, day out to put your foot all the way down to the floor if you don't want to tear the guts out of the gearbox.' His aversion to the past was as strong as ever and their early life together was now the past.

'I'm sorry. I didn't think.'

'Well, start to think now. Did you *ever* think, I'd like to ask. Blessed will be the day when you do start to think.' His exasperation blazed on its own impetus and she did not challenge. She drove slowly on in the rain, wishing the car would never reach Cox's Hill when she would have to change gears again.

One wet day it was she who proposed that they go to Strandhill for the day. She hoped to allay his restlessness. He scoffed at the idea at first but then suddenly agreed to go. They took a flask of tea and sandwiches. They walked part of the links. They looked at shops. They sat in the car, drank tea and watched the ocean falling. Before they left he insisted playfully that they walk down to the tideline. There he stooped to put his hand in the last spent run of a wave and brought it to his lips to taste the salt and then gave it to Rose to taste as well.

'Well, that was a nice outing.' There was a note of relief in Rose's voice when they got home.

'It was better than being cooped up in the house all day for nothing.'

On the next outing they went north across the border to Enniskillen. Increasingly they leaned on these outings to escape the claustrophobia of the interminable day. They were shut up in days. Gradually they visited all the towns and places Nell Morahan and Michael had passed indolent days in years before.

The changeless image of itself that the house so fiercely held to was now being threatened in small ways by the different reality the untutored and uncaring outside world saw. Instead of passing the day in Strandhill or Enniskillen Moran decided to go into the bank to get the manager's advice on whether to sell or keep certain government bonds he held.

When Rose and Moran went to the counter to ask to see the manager none of the staff knew who either of them were. They were asked to sit down and wait outside the manager's office.

'You'd think we were looking for Confession on Christmas Eve,' Moran complained to Rose after a long while had passed. 'It can't be long now. There must be some business keeping him.'

When the manager emerged he was in affable conversation with a customer as he courteously showed him to the main entrance. One of the counter staff indicated the old couple waiting on the chairs. When he returned he asked them into the office. He was tall and grey haired and did not know them. As he was searching for Moran's file, a girl knocked and entered with a cup and saucer. They could smell the coffee. Two fig roll biscuits were balanced on the rim of the saucer. Then the phone rang. As soon as the manager discovered who the caller was he abandoned his search for the file and pulled his chair up to the desk. A long conversation began about a golf club election during which the manager ate both fig rolls and drank the cup of coffee. Several times Rose looked anxiously at Moran. If this had happened when they first met he would have been up and out of both office and bank long ago. Instead he continued sitting dejectedly and a little tiredly, not looking around him. He was still there when the manager put down the phone and apologized. Somehow he seemed to think that their business had been concluded and proceeded to show them out the door quite graciously. They left without a word. Once out on the pavement it was Rose who was beside herself with anger.

'I never saw such manners in all my life.'

'Who cares anyhow?' Moran said. 'Nobody cares.'

'I care,' she said passionately.

'That doesn't count. Nobody bothers these days.'

At the weekend Rose complained so much about the incident to Mona that Mona grew enraged. She was intent on taking the Monday off and going to the bank to attack the manager.

'I'm telling you there was a time he wouldn't have done that to Daddy. By the time I'm finished with him he'll know something. And I'll report him.'

'Don't waste a day on him,' Rose now found herself counselling. 'Let it go. If he's that ignorant, you'd only be contributing to his education,' she began her old laugh.

'There was a time Daddy would have brought him up fairly short.'

'I'm going to report him,' Mona said. But she never did.

During the long nights as he once again added up the monies that he had or wrote to Michael or Michael's wife or one of the girls, he kept repeating to Rose how he felt that he had only really failed with one of his children and that it troubled him more than any of his other dealings throughout his life.

'I think he feels I did him some wrong or harm.'

'You know that's not true. Luke always took those things too personally. Differences take place in every family but no one pays heed to them the way he does,' Rose said.

'I'd like to see him but I know he won't come. I have nothing against him. For my part I forgive him everything. If I write him that, at least I'll feel that the fault won't be mine. He won't be on my conscience.'

He spent several nights writing the letter. Some of his old fire and anger returned as he wrote. The finished letter was short. He did not show it to Rose. 'There are times in my life when I have pondered my sanity,' it began. ' "They are all mad but me and thee and I have doubts of me." Rose thinks that we are as good or bad as anyone in life and my life is now too short to keep a grudge, real or imaginary. My present capabilities are of little matter. Let me say I had no wish to harm you in the past and I have no wish to harm you in the future and if I have done so in thought, word or deed I am sorry. The daffodils are nearly in bloom, also shrubs, flowers, fruit, etc. It'll soon be time for planting. Tired now and of that thought, who cares anyhow? Daddy.'

He must be dying, Luke thought after he read the letter. He put it aside at first but then after rereading it he felt the same for Moran as he would feel for any mortal and wrote back in kind. He felt no bitterness or reproach. There was nothing to forgive. He was sorry and asked to be forgiven for any hurt he had caused. It is not what he wants but it will have to do, he thought.

Maggie rang to say that she was going home and wanted Luke to go with her. They were all going to Great Meadow for Monaghan Day. 'Daddy is not well. Do you remember in the long ago when McQuaid used to come to the house for Monaghan Day? We feel it could give Daddy heart again if we were there. Rose said he was so much better after we were all there for Christmas.'

'I'd be no use,' Luke said. 'I can't go.'

'He wants to see you.'

'He wrote me a letter.'

'I know.'

'I wrote him back.'

'He didn't get that letter yet.'

176

'I wrote him as he wrote me. I have no bitterness. I have nothing.'

'Why can't you come home with us then?'

'I'd be no use. We don't get on.'

'You never really tried.'

'It's too late now.'

'You're no help. You're no help to us at all.'

Moran did not lack for attention. All the girls came to the house and came again and again. They planned and arranged the entire summer so that Rose was as little on her own as possible. Michael and his wife and their two children came in August. Once the summer ended Mona came every single weekend from Dublin. Sheila also came whenever she could. Moran grew weaker. He had a number of small strokes. They began to feel that this once powerful man who was such an integral part of their lives could slip away from them at any time into the air. They all came for Christmas and then they decided to come again at the end of February to revive Monaghan Day. They explained to Rose how McQuaid used to come to the house for a grand tea, recalling the nervousness, the excitement, the glory of the stories, the whiskey McQuaid drank.

Rose was doubtful about the idea from the beginning. She could not see how any miracle could be managed by the simple revival of a day she herself had never heard about until now but the girls clung so much to the idea that Rose felt she couldn't stand in their way. They wanted it to be a surprise. Against all reason they felt they could turn his slow decline around to bring back all his old spirit in one bound.

They came for Monaghan Day. They brought him gloves for his cold hands. Acknowledging that they had come distances for him, he broke his embargo on the past and spoke of the war and McQuaid and the lost Monaghan Days. At the end of the Rosary that wrapped up the day, he prayed for James McQuaid's soul; but the attempt to revive Moran with the day had been futile.

The failure to change anything only strengthened their determination not to let him slip from them. They began to be in Great Meadow more than in their own homes. Muted complaints about neglected children, the mounting cost of Maggie's air fares, had to be faced; but they grew so upset when faced with anything that interfered with their concern for Moran that the charges were always let drop, for when faced with their deep turmoil it was easier to let commonsensical objections out the window: air fares could be paid for later, lost hours worked. They were so bound together by the illness that they felt close to being powerful together. Such was the strength of the instinct that they felt that they could force their beloved to remain in life if only they could, together, turn his will around. Since they had the power of birth there was no reason why they couldn't will this life free of death. For the first time in his life Moran began to fear them.

'You'll have to shape up, Daddy. You'll just have to pull yourself together and get better.'

'Who cares? Who cares anyhow?'

All they felt he had to do was to turn his life over to them and they would will him back to health again. It ran counter to the way he had managed his own life. He had never in all his life bowed in anything to a mere Other. Now he wanted to escape, to escape the house, the room, their insistence that he get better, his illness. The first time he went missing there was panic. They searched the bathroom, all the other rooms, and when they reached the stone hallway they saw that the front door was open.

They found him leaning in exhaustion on a wooden post at the back of the house, staring into the emptiness of the meadow. He did not speak as they led him back to the house. They thought it was a wayward fit of delinquency to test their vigilance. They watched him more closely after that but there were times when he slipped out to the fields in spite of their care and always in the same direction. Past the old pear tree in brilliant white blossom against the wall, last year's nettles withered and tangled in the abandoned mowing machine beneath the tree, the corrugated roof of the lean-to he had built as a workshop for wet days, and on to the meadow. It was no longer empty but filling with a fresh growth, a faint blue tinge in the rich green of the young grass. To die was never to look on all this again. It would live in others' eyes but not in his. He had never realized when he was in the midst of confident life what an amazing glory he was part of. He heard his name being called frantically. Then he was scolded and led back to the house. He stopped stubbornly before the door. 'I never knew how hard it is to die,' he said simply.

One day later the priest came to the house to hear his Confession, to give him Communion and Extreme Unction. 'I never met a priest yet who wasn't afraid of death. What do you think that means?' he said to Rose.

'Maybe that's why they become priests.'

'What good does that do them?'

'They make sure of their own place in heaven that way.'

'Then they shouldn't be afraid to die.'

'I suppose everybody is afraid.'

'If they believed what they preach they shouldn't be afraid. Who knows anyhow? Who cares?'

One evening when Mona was sitting by his bed thinking he was asleep he surprised her by asking, 'Do you think I am finished, Mona?'

'Of course not,' she chided, surprised. 'You're going to have to work at it though if you want us to get you better. Trying to go out to look at the meadow is no help at all.'

Late one night Mona said to Rose, 'I wonder why Daddy wants so much to get to the meadow. He's always looking out at the same place. He must see something there.' And without meaning to both women suddenly began to cry.

The girls had to return to their own homes. He worsened. The brown habit was bought and brought into the house and hidden. When the girls came back and saw the state he was in they lost all thought of ever leaving the house again while he lived. They sent for Michael and he came with his son.

There are some who struggle and rave on the edge of dying, others who make a great labour of it like a difficult birth, but

Moran slipped evenly out of life. He just faded away in front of their eyes. They were all gathered around him.

'Why aren't you praying?' he demanded as if he knew he was slipping away.

They immediately dropped to their knees around the bed.

'Thou, O Lord, wilt open my lips,' Rose began.

Tears slipped down their faces as they repeated the 'Our Fathers' and 'Hail Marys'. Maggie had begun her Mystery when it grew clear that Moran was trying to speak. She stopped and the room was still. The low whisper was unmistakable: '*Shut up!*' They looked at one another in fear and confusion but Rose nodded vigorously to Maggie to ignore the whispered command and to continue. She managed to struggle back into the rhythm of the prayers when Mona cried out, 'Daddy's gone!' They got up off their knees and stood over the bed. Weeping loudly Maggie and Sheila embraced one another and Mona ran angrily from the room, slamming doors on the way, shouting, 'That doctor shouldn't have been let give him that injection this morning.' Rose turned to Maggie, 'Would you mind going after Mona to see that she's all right. I think that must be Michael's car I hear turning in at the gate.'

Some of the anger at the death veered towards Michael as soon as he appeared in the hallway. Being left on the periphery of what was happening he had become bored and driven to town with his son. 'You're a nice gentleman. You couldn't even manage to be in the house when Daddy was going.' He did not realize at first what had taken place and put up his hands in jocose surrender to these fierce and impossible women but went very pale and still as soon as he understood that his father had just died. Gently Rose opened the door to the room and he nodded silently to her and went in. Then she took his son by the hand. The child and woman went from room to room until they had stopped each clock in the house and covered every mirror.

It was a blessing that so many practical things had to be quickly attended to. Word had to be sent to Woods to come and lay out the body. Whiskey and sherry and stout had to be bought for callers, sandwiches made, the priest and the doctor to be notified. Rose insisted on going herself to the undertakers. She looked at all the coffins in the showroom and picked the most expensive, a beautiful oak casket. A grave had to be dug. There was an argument between the girls over whether or not Luke should be notified. A telegram was sent but he neither replied nor came.

When Woods came to the house the Franciscan habit was taken from its hiding place. The door to the room was closed while he laid the body out. His Rosary beads were taken from the little black purse and twined through his fingers clasped together on the breast of the brown habit.

In ones and twos callers trickled to the stilled house all that evening. They murmured 'Sorry' as they shook hands with Rose and Michael and the three girls, blessed themselves as they entered the room, knelt by the foot of the bed to pray, and touched the dead hands or forehead in a gesture of leave-taking when they rose. They then sat on chairs by the bed and were offered whiskey or beer or wine or tea. Few of the callers had ever been in the house before and they looked about them with unabashed curiosity.

All through the night they kept vigil by his side. Time should have stopped with the clocks but instead it moved in a glazed dream of tiredness without their ticking insistence. Morning stole over the fields. The callers continued coming to the house throughout the day. At six the body would be taken to the church. As it drew closer to six the minutes seemed to race.

The hearse was coming, turning at the wooden gate. A row of cars had gathered out on the road. The empty coffin was taken in. The house was closed.

They all had to go into the room to look on him a last time. They would never see him in the world again but he was already gone from them. The coffin was then brought into the room and laid on chairs beside the bed. The room was closed. Someone started a Decade of the Rosary and it was taken up by those standing between the flowerbeds of the little lawn just outside the door. A cry sounded from within the house as the heavy closed coffin was edged slowly out of the room. The front door was opened. The coffin was carried to the open door of the hearse. The hearse crawled out to the iron gate and turned right under the yew. All that night the coffin would lie before the high altar, only a few feet away from where he had waited so impatiently for his best man the day he had married Rose.

It was a heartbreakingly lovely May evening when they returned from the church but they couldn't bear to walk about among the trees in the light. They went round the house to let up the blinds one by one and then they made tea.

'My hand feels as if it's been through a wringer,' Mona said.

'Mine is no better. I thought the line would never end. Some of the hands were like shovels,' Sheila said.

'They like to give you a really good friendly healthy shake,' Rose was the most in control, even now laughing her low, humorous laugh. 'They feel you might think they didn't mean it if it wasn't a good hard friendly shake.'

'The poor devils mean well,' Michael said combatively but it was let go by.

More arrangements needed to be seen to. Sean and Sheila's children were coming in the morning for the funeral. A discussion started as to where they would sleep if they decided to stay overnight. Sheila said before the conversation got properly under way that they would all definitely be going back after the funeral. They were all numb with tiredness but no one wanted to go to bed. They continued talking and making cups of tea as if they were afraid to let go of the day.

After morning High Mass they buried him in a new plot beneath a yew tree. The birds sang in their territories high in the branches of oak and ash and evergreen, and little wrens and robins flitted hither and thither along the low graveyard wall. The Plains were bathed in sunshine and in all the fields between the stone walls the unhoused cattle were grazing greedily on the early grass.

All through High Mass and the slow funeral a faded tricolour covered the coffin; and as the casket stood on the edge of the grave a little man in a brown felt hat, old and stiff enough to have fought with Fionn and Oisin came out of the crowd. With deep respect he removed his hat before folding the worn flag and with it he stepped back into the crowd. There was no firing party.

As the shining ornamented oak coffin was lowered with ropes, a whisper loud enough to cause heads to turn in the crowd was heard: 'That man would have died to see so much money go down with him into the ground.'

Two local politicians who had vied with one another for prominence all through the funeral now fell back from the crowd as the prayers began. They walked away to the boundary wall and leaned together out over the stones in amiable conspiratorial camaraderie, sometimes turning their heads to look back to the crowd gathered about the grave in undisguised contempt.

Rose, surrounded by the girls, left the graveside. Michael stood a little way off with his son beside Sean Flynn and Mark O'Donoghue who had come all the way from London. Age had taken the Elvis look off Mark and except for his weathered face he could have been another civil servant like Sean. The men followed the bereaved women out of the graveyard at a hesitant, respectful distance, unsure of their place in the mourning.

But as the small tight group of stricken women slowly left the graveyard they seemed with every step to be gaining in strength. It was as if their first love and allegiance had been pledged uncompromisingly to this one house and man and that they knew that he had always been at the very living centre of all parts of their lives. Now not only had they never broken that pledge but they were renewing it for a second time with this other woman who had come in among them and married him. Their continual homecomings had been an affirmation of its unbroken presence, and now, as they left him under the yew, it was as if each of them in their different ways had become Daddy.

'He may be gone home but he'll always be with us,' Maggie spoke for them all. 'He'll never leave us now.'

'Poor Daddy,' Rose echoed absently out of her own thoughts before waking and turning brightly towards the girls.

At the gate they paused firmly to wait for the men who lagged well behind on the path and were chatting and laughing pleasantly together, their children around them.

'Will you look at the men. They're more like a crowd of women,' Sheila said, remarking on the slow frivolity of their pace. 'The way Michael, the skit, is getting Sean and Mark to laugh you'd think they were coming from a dance.'